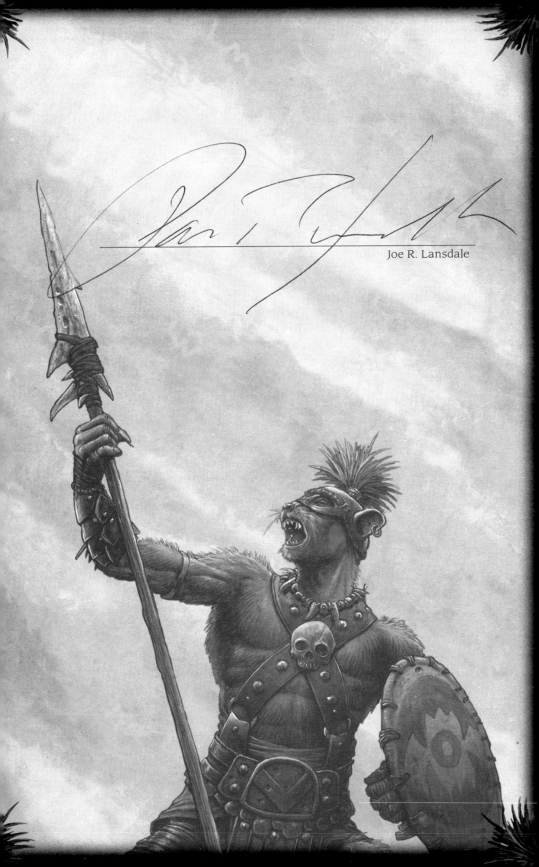

Joe R. Lansdale

THE SKY DONE
RIPPED

THE SKY DONE RIPPED

A Ned the Seal Adventure

by

JOE R. LANSDALE

Subterranean Press • 2019

First Edition

ISBN
978-1-59606-910-7

Subterranean Press
PO Box 190106
Burton, MI 48519

subterraneanpress.com

Manufactured in the United States of America.

This one is for good seals everywhere. All those members of the Ned the Seal fan club please put on your red fezzes and clap like a seal. And, we're off. Fish will be served at noon.

In Preparation for Events to Come

This comes later, but let's look at it now.

Mountains covered in trees. A view from below the mountains, a city on the banks of a great river. And the people look out and up, and what do they see?

Metal machines rolling on massive and multiple sets of stone and wood wheels, squeaking like legions of mice, grinding earth and trees and folks and bones to dust, squirting pulpy knots of blood like strawberry jelly. The screams of the dying mix with the squeak of the wheels as they roll over flesh and bone. And behind them, everywhere they have been, the earth is made barren and smoke rises up from multiple fires.

The sky is bright and the ground is red. The air trembles.

And the grinders roll on.

———◆———

The frightened people think: Here they come and here She comes, She Who Must Be Obeyed and Eats Lunch Early. They had heard of her by runner, carrier pigeon, and a weird old lady who said she had visions but was mostly thought of as drunk. No one ever believed her, but damnit, she was always right.

Final analysis:

Hitch up your drawers and run like hell.

Squeak and crunch, grind and squirt. The machines won't stop. The mighty ones come with their mighty queen and all her slaves.

Hide your men. Hide your women. Hide your children. Hide your supplies. Flee to the forests. Run like hell. Already people are dead and dying for miles and miles, and the ground is being paved with corpses and everything in the great army's path is knocked down and smoked by fires.

Out of the mountain shadows they still come, rolling bright and shiny beneath the constant sun, a juggernaut of certain death and destruction, slavery and humiliation, and a bad change in diet.

And so, for now we move away, to the present, but we'll be back. Or to be more correct, we'll be forward.

Part One:

In which we learn nothing about Bongo Bill's nickname but think we are going to, and we meet a lot of different sorts of folks, one horrible villain, and of course a plucky seal named Ned. Heads up. Watch out for dinosaurs.

One

From the Journal of Him Who Would Come to Be Known as Bongo Bill

Strangeness and Irony.
You'll see what I mean.
When all this happened, I was a precocious eighteen.

I have always been afraid of deep water, of the great oceans, seas and gulfs. I fear drowning. The idea of floating down, down, down to the bottomless ocean gives me the willies. Makes me see dark swirly-blue, makes my hair feel wet, even if I am only thinking about it.

So, guess what?

I found myself at sea.

It was the Gulf of Mexico, actually, at least that's where it started. Later there was the Atlantic, and then all that ice, a hole in another world, and a drift down under. And I don't mean Australia.

But the ship at sea. That's where the serious stuff started for me. That's where the oddness and danger caught up with me.

Pull away for a moment, and let's go back farther, let's start at another place instead of on the ship. This is the prelude to it all.

Six months earlier the flying saucers came (technically, not all of them were saucer shaped, but that's what they were called) and they leaked out disease, and they did it on purpose. It washed down from the skies and was carried on the wind, a bacterial nastiness that first hit Canada, a big-ass dose that knocked most of the Canadians flat.

As the disease soared down, it gained momentum because the germs liked warmth, and the winds were blowing fast toward the south. By the time it hit the southern part of the U.S. it was wild as a jungle beast.

The symptoms of the disease were brutal. It ate your windpipe, it made you squirt shit. It boiled your brain and steamed your eyes. It made your bones turn brittle and finally become mush. The insides of your mouth crackled with electricity. It turned humans into screaming, squirming worms. I heard the dying smelled like hot dog breath. A few got the jiggers with their dose of disease, which was a kind of dance their contaminated brains made them do. Hop-along-dying is what it was. One moment the infected are hopping, then the next moment, not so much. Did a stiff-legged boogie then hit the dirt. I don't think I mentioned that steam came out of their mouths, noses and ears and around the eyes, but it did. It made people swell. Bellies burst, pants ripped, torn apart by cosmically diseased farts. Rumors were, it blew out the male and female sex organs. Don't know all the details on that. Don't want to.

So, me and my mother and father, and little sister, Suzie Q, were part of a lucky few who had government connections. My father worked for the President of the United States, who was partly responsible for what happened. The president was a dunderhead. The saucers came and the aliens offered us all manner of sweetness and freedom from war and disease, so President Dunderhead (not his real name, but certainly an appropriate moniker) took a shot at them, and over Canadian territory at that. A big fat rocket was fired, missed a saucer and took out Montreal.

That's how the president was. Shoot first, ask questions later. Just ask his three wives. They had been sperm-targets and had birthed children almost as hollow as he was. President Dunderhead probably didn't know where the U.S. ended and Canada began. Bottom line, he turned a magnificent peace offering from an all-powerful alien presence into war. So instead of curing our diseases, the aliens waggled tentacles and snapped their beaks and pulled levers, or pushed buttons, or whatever the hell they did, and gave us a disease, and boy what a doozy it was.

Still, and this is where some of that irony fits in, I owe President Dunderhead my life because my father worked for him. Dunderhead didn't really know my father well. Dad worked as a chef at the White House. The President really liked my father's cooking. My dad could boil a turnip and somehow manage to have it taste like a Frenchman's delight. Thing was, though, Dad said Dunderhead didn't know a thing about fine cuisine, and Dad figured out pretty quick to blacken his steaks and feed him French fries and burgers, give him beer and lots of pie and pudding, mostly served on a tray in bed. President Dunderhead was so happy he'd fall asleep early, which was a temporary blessing for the country and the world. I think he dreamed of where he could next stamp his presidential seal. Already it was on his golf tees, his underwear (visible through his thin white golfing pants in a famous photo of his broad, stretched ass) and some said that presidential seal was tattooed on his wife's ass near the hole. That could just be rumor, though.

The problem was when he was awake. Like when he authorized the attack on the flying saucers. We managed to shoot one down after we took out Montreal, and President Dunderhead was proud of that. He'd call one a hundred, and two three hundred. He was long on ego and short on math.

Let me note that many missiles missed aliens and blew away other spots in Canada.

Yippie, said Dunderhead.

He didn't like Canada anyway.

Thing was, those who worked for the president (or at least some, the tightest in the inner circle) got the chance to get the hell out of Dodge, and we saddled up. Obviously, this included families. We took trains and planes and automobiles, but the planes didn't fly right anymore. It's odd, but it had something to do with the disease. It filled the air of the North American continent and clogged jet engines like invisible wads of steel wool. So, there was very little flying, at least in the diseased areas, which were expanding.

You'd think everyone would have the disease, but some were immune. Something different in their genetics, I suppose. And there was the vaccination U.S. scientists came up with. You see, we, the chosen ones, had an inoculation based on the blood of the immune, and it worked like a charm. Some smart people had figured it out, and fast, but not fast enough to save the bulk of Canada, or most of the U.S., especially the working class who didn't have quick escape access. U.S. President Dunderhead didn't want to distribute the vaccine to anyone other than those he chose.

He always said he was a president of the people, but as it turned out, not the poor people, not most people.

He said in private, "Who are they anyway? They aren't rich."

He was right. They weren't.

But, I come back to this. We, because of President Dunderhead, who didn't know his asshole from a hole in the ground, the scientists who invented the serum, and my father's cooking, survived.

We didn't do the jiggers or turn into wormy flesh or get blown up in a whirl of shit and a stench of farts.

As Dunderhead said, "Disease is for the other people."

We didn't have the disease to worry about, but the saucer folk still had death rays, beams of blue light that lit up buildings and turned humans into charred stick figures, and finally puffs of black smoke. If the disease didn't get you, the ray guns would. Snap, crackle, flame and pop.

We got out of Dodge (Washington).

We flew out on a private jet, ahead of the wind, ahead of the disease, but jets could only be trusted to go so far. As I said, all the air was starting to clog up with that alien stuff. We had to land and get off the jet and go by sea, had to catch a big, fat cruise ship down Galveston, Texas way.

The war ships were already gone, as was most of the Navy, not to mention the rest of the military, outside of a few armed forces folk here and there, mostly wandering around in circles. So, we didn't have destroyers or any other sort of military water ride, not even a water ski on loan from Navy SEALs. A paddle boat from a water park.

But we had cruise ships.

There were several of them, and they were all full of Dunderhead's personal picks; the people he cared about, or like my father, someone who could prepare something he liked to eat.

On one ship there were a number of non-government folk, mostly young women. I had an idea what that was about. Dunderhead loosely referred to it as the cream pie boat.

Dunderhead said the ships had plenty of frozen steak and hamburger meat and hamburger buns on board. He seemed excited by the idea. There was also an onboard golf course. You would have thought he was taking us all on holiday the way he gloated and pranced and made faces that would shame a monkey. Later, it was learned someone had forgotten to pack mustard on board, which was a letdown for a lot of us.

To get on the ships you had to have a red badge. Blue for the young women. As I said, they had a special ship. Anyone else who tried to board was shot. No badge, no sailing.

My entire family had red badges. Our ship was leaving for New Zealand. I'm not sure why New Zealand.

I just remember a simple announcement.

"We're going to New Zealand."

Okay.

Some said the New Zealanders had become the leaders of the world and had a very large air force, as did New Guinea. It was bragged about. I guess they hadn't considered that whole disease thing and what it could do to an air force. Maybe they had plans to thwart that.

Also, I think they did have the largest air force by then, but it was a handful of prop planes and an ultra-light. I saw a photo of the ultra-light. It looked like a lawn mower motor and a lawn chair with wings mounted on it. It had a little machine gun fastened on the front and the propeller rotated in such a way the gun could be fired rapidly without pinging off the blades. Of course, the machine gun would have had about as much effect on the saucers as blowing peas through a straw.

We got on the ship in the middle of the night, and there were other ships in sight, maybe half a dozen. Our escape flotilla was set to go.

And so, what was left of the United States government, as well as its cook staff, and all their families, and boats full of nubile young women, took out across the water, a version of "Life Is But a Dream" playing on speakers in cabins and hallways, soft and sleepy sounding, like the world was all right.

During the lifejacket and lifeboat drill, I could see the water and I realized we were moving rapidly because the lights of the shore were going away. Seeing those lights growing smaller, and the water and

the sky so dark, frightened me to the core. The dusky water and the dark night met and made a ball of shadow around our ship as the lights retreated and the night grew firm.

The ship used very little illumination as we made our escape. The ship was guided by means of instruments that saw through the dark, pointed the correct direction with arrows and blips.

Now and again we saw the distant lights of saucers in the sky, but either the aliens didn't see us, or they had bigger plans. After a short time, we didn't see the saucers anymore. Where once they lit up the night sky like lightning bugs, the sky was empty now, except for the stars and the moon and the dark between them.

Where had they gone?

Well, I didn't know the answer to that at the time, and what answer I do know may be flawed. In the end it didn't matter.

The days and nights passed at sea. I imagined I could hear them pass, hour by hour, like a thudding of the cosmos trying to realign itself.

Two

"Can you swim?" said Tomi, a girl on board the ship.

It was night again, and our whole family was on deck near the railing looking out at the water. There was no moon and it was dark, except for a modicum of orangish lights along the deck next to the railing, under the overhang that was the upper level. There were several levels. It was thought those lights would not be noticed by air, protecting us from the saucers' view. I thought that was wishful thinking. I think the truth was the nearly complete darkness finally wore on our fearless leader, that's what I thought. He most likely said, "Let there be light, even if it's dimmed light," and there was.

We could hear the Atlantic slopping at the sides of the ship. The air smelled of salt and dead fish and anytime someone opened a door to the deck, the odor of greasy French fries drifted out to us, and then to sea, possible filling the gills of fish with cholesterol.

I had to talk to Dad about those fries. What the fuck kind of cooking oil was he using?

This night I was standing off a short way from my family, next to Tomi, because my parents mistakenly thought I liked her, or would want to be around another person my age. I would almost rather have been on a saucer with the aliens with my ass cheeks spread by extraterrestrial salad tongs with an anal drill descending.

Tomi was the President's daughter. His other two kids were on another cruise ship. Tomi roamed the decks like a wolf seeking out a wounded caribou. We had crossed paths at the White House and I thought she was a dick, which considering she didn't have one was quite a feat. My opinion of her hadn't improved with disease and alien invasion. She had a face that looked perfect to shit on and a smile that looked perfect to knock to shatters.

I know how that sounds. But, she was a bully, big and mean, and I was me, and at that point, me wasn't much. We'll come back to how me shook out later. You can decide if I gained my worth. Right then I was all a-tremble, worried sick, fearful of water and flying saucers, and when Tomi was around I was even more nervous. She had already beaten my ass a couple of times, just to show she could. Kicked me in the hallway, pushed me down some ship stairs, followed me into a general bathroom to punch me in the head.

She said me, "Tell me you like it."

"But I don't," I said.

"Tell me you do."

"Why would I do that?"

"Do it," and she punched me again, knocking me down on the slimy bathroom floor.

"I like it," I said.

"See there," she said. "Told you that you did."

"You told me to say it."

She kicked me and I said how much I liked it again. I said it loud and happy sounding. I was starting to believe it. She was also a bit of a firebug, as the burnt-down West Wing of the White House had proven. She struck matches and flicked them at me so she could watch me hop.

I thought later, when I was safer, next time she does that I'm going to punch her and shove that box of matches down her throat.

I knew that was some bullshit.

As I said. She was her and I was me, and me was nothing to fear.

So, she got to keep her shitable face and her punchable teeth, and I became highly vigilant; a mouse in a house full of cats couldn't have been more vigilant.

I haven't forgotten my mention of Tomi's question. She asked if I could swim. I hadn't answered right away. I thought it might be a trick question.

"You hearing me, knucklehead?" she said. "You afraid of the water? I heard you were afraid of the water, bitch."

"Who told you that?"

"Your mother."

Goddamnit, Mom.

"She said that's why you stand so far from the rail. And you should. End up in that water, you'll be dead in minutes. Water's cold and deep and the waves are high. You aren't much of a swimmer, and out there, you can kiss your wet, hypothermic ass goodbye."

"I have a lifejacket."

Unlike Tomi, I was wearing my jacket. So was my sister, who had wandered down the deck a piece and was leaning over the railing looking out at the ocean. My parents were positioned between us, holding hands, thinking, I'm sure, about what was next. They were not wearing lifejackets. Their clothes whipped in the wind.

Tomi was still chattering.

"Even in a jacket, you'll just float and freeze. Lot of sharks out there too. They say this is a serious place for them. They wouldn't mind a Bill Boy popsicle."

That made me really nervous, her talking about drowning in the ocean, my biggest fear, and then mentioning sharks, my second greatest fear, right next to public speaking and tight pants and Tomi herself.

The thought of deep water and sharks made my bowels loose, so guess what? There was a loud grating noise and the ship heaved high up and splashed down hard enough my teeth snapped together. I grabbed at a rack against the deck wall, a rack that held a life preserver on a peg. The preserver was round like a doughnut, orange in color.

The ship tilted. Tomi lost her footing, slid along the deck and went through an exit gap in the railing that was blocked only by a thin chain that connected one side of the railing to the other. She slid right under that chain.

As she went through that gap toward the ocean, there in the dim lights that ran along the deck, I could see her eyes. They were wide and I heard her yell as she shot from sight, "Rat fuck."

I waved bye-bye to her, and then she was in the water and gone.

I thought, swim you bitch, swim.

Three

The ship tilted even more.

I thought: For heaven's sake, someone lower a lifeboat.

That wasn't going to happen, however. The ship was sinking, going down fast and I had no idea why.

I saw my mother and father sliding along the deck past me, heading to where the bow was slanting and dipping. My little sister Suzie Q slid toward me. I leaned out from the deck wall, still clutching the buoy rack, and grabbed hold of her lifejacket.

I had her.

Last sight I had of my parents was them sliding down the deck. My mother was looking back at us. The little lights along the deck showed the fright in her eyes. I think that fright was for us more than herself or my father. What's going to happen to my babies, I bet she was thinking.

I never got to ask her.

Her hands waved spasmodically. It looked like nothing less than an enthusiastic greeting. I think she yelled something. If she did, the wind caught it up and took it away, and the ship kept dipping.

I knew enough from reading about ship disasters, which was a hobby of mine associated with my fear of vast water, to know that me and Suzie Q were as screwed as our parents if we stayed on board the ship.

I was to experience my first real courageous event. Perhaps it was merely desperation, but I think it may have been a moment of change. A new me swelling up inside the old me.

I grabbed Suzie Q and kicked away from the wall, pulling the buoy off the rack as we went. We began to slide down deck, but I managed to claw and kick us closer to the rail.

What I remember then was looking out from the slanting ship and seeing the ocean was very close. The water was leaping and I could taste salt on my tongue, feel it burning in my nostrils. I managed to get to my feet, leaning at a mean angle, still clutching the buoy and Suzie Q.

I just let us fall over the side. We bounced against the ship as we fell, protected a little by our lifejackets, and then we hit the dark sea. We were only a few feet from the sinking ship, and as it went down it created a suction, and we went down with it into icy wet blackness.

Tell Davy Jones to save us a spot in his locker.

Four

Iblacked out.

I don't know how long we were under the water. All I know is, thankfully, we bobbed back up. We were both alive, spitting and coughing freezing salt water. The round, orange life preserver was gone, but we still had our jackets on, though mine had been pushed up under my chin so hard it felt like I had been punched. I shoved it down. I remembered reading that if you drank salt water, it could make you crazy. It seemed like something worth remembering right then.

I made an important mental note. Don't drink salt water. Keep coughing it out.

I figured when it got right down to it, it didn't matter. The water, as Tomi had said, was frigid. We probably only had minutes before we died of hypothermia.

Oh yeah. It might be death by sharks, but they were going to have to hurry if they wanted a hot meal.

The cruise ship was not completely under. We had come up not too far from it, but far enough that we were no longer feeling the suction. I had no idea why we had survived. I saw the ship's dim deck lights at the stern, and I could see some of the lights shining under water. I thought, hell, a saucer could have easily seen us at sea. Chalk another black mark up for President Dunderhead and his plans.

Speaking of flying saucers.

I saw what the ship had hit.

Surprise. A flying saucer. It was massive, larger than the giant cruise ship, and it was floating in the water as if made of Styrofoam.

The ship went down under. The saucer continued to float, and suddenly I realized why we had not stayed under the waves.

We were standing on something.

Five

The thing we were standing on rose from beneath the waves and we were lifted completely out of the water. The air hit us, and I felt even colder than when we were in the ocean. Suzie Q, looking stunned, was shaking violently, and in a moment, so was I.

What we were standing on was invisible. There didn't seem to be anything there, but there was, because our feet were on something solid.

For an instant, I thought perhaps I was hallucinating. Thought I was still thrashing about in the dark ocean, but even as that thought was flowing through my mind, the support beneath us became visible as it rose higher out of the sea.

It was very wide. There was a kind of hum and a bit of a glow, and then I could see we were standing on what looked like metal, shiny and yellow as fresh baby shit. Waves crashed along the sides of our support, which I determined was rounded on the sides and flat on top.

Then a part of the shiny metal hissed and a lid flew up and a trap door was revealed. Light shone from it, and it was a strong light. The light went up into the night like a laser blast.

I struggled toward the light and the opening, trying not to slip on the slick surface, dragging Suzie Q after me, because by this time she had passed out. I feared she was near death due to the cold.

When I reached the gap in the craft beneath us, I could feel warmth coming out of it. Inside the craft was a ladder on one side of the hole, which was quite wide, and on the other side was a plastic slide. I pulled us toward the slide, sat on my ass, pulled Suzie Q after me, and down we went. The hatch closed up above us with a hiss and a snapping sound.

We landed on some soft padding. I thought we were inside an alien ship, like the one we had crashed into. I was expecting ass probes and semen samples collected by big-eyed aliens, but right then, to be out of the water was helpful. I wanted to quit shivering. I wanted to save Suzie Q. I wanted a whole list of things, but mostly I wanted to be warm and dry, and I wanted something to eat.

And then I saw at the far end of the matting we had landed on, holding a thermos with a flipper, and I swear, a thumb attached to that flipper, was a large seal wearing a red fez with a tassel.

I shook my head to rid myself of the hallucination.

Nope. Still there.

Still holding the thermos in one thumb-enhanced flipper, the seal held up, with his other flipper and thumb, a slate.

Written on the slate was: HI. I'M NED. I HAVE HOT SOUP.

Six

Suzie Q had come around by this time and was marveling at the arrival of a seal wearing a fez.

The seal filled the cup that came off the top of the thermos. It was a large cup, and it took almost half the soup. He gave that to Suzie Q, and the rest to me so I could drink directly from the thermos. We drank the soup like cold water, even though it was hot. It was a kind of fish soup.

Suzie Q looked at Ned and giggled.

"I love your hat," she said.

Ned wrote on the slate.

ME TOO. I FEEL STYLISH.

When we finished the soup, and felt strong enough to stand, the seal wiped his slate and wrote again with a greasy, black pencil.

FOLLOW ME FOR WARM CLOTHES.

What I had not noticed initially was that Ned was riding on a kind of sled. It hovered over the floor and moved silently. We followed behind his sled and into a hallway. There were doors all along the wall in the hall. One of the doors was open, and we went through that into a large well-furnished room. The furniture was Victorian in design.

Ned pointed a flipper at some drawers that were built into the wall and made a barking noise.

I went to the drawers and opened them one at a time. They were packed with clothes.

Ned was writing on his slate again. When I came back over he had written:

THERE ARE TWO ROOMS. THEY CONNECT. PICK ONE APIECE. GET DRY. CHANGE CLOTHES. COME OUT THE DOOR AND TAKE A RIGHT. YOU WILL FIND US.

Then away Ned went.

"He's cute," Suzie Q said.

I left Suzie Q in the first room, went through a connecting door into another. My room looked just like the other room. I found a bathroom and relieved myself and took a long hot shower, and while wrapped in a towel, I looked through the drawers for clothes.

There was a pair of clown britches, and unfortunately, they were the only things that fit. They were orange and green with blue trim at the bottom of the legs. There was also a clown hairdo. One of those wild hair fringes that fastened on the head with an elastic strap and was colored green. I decided I didn't need that.

I found a loose blue T-shirt that had a logo on the front. PIPPO'S FISH AND CHIPS. I put that on. I found some fluffy orange socks and some lace-up boots that looked as if they would fit.

I took the clothes into the bathroom and put them on and looked at myself in the mirror. My fur was standing up on my face, so I dampened my fingers under the sink faucet and slicked it down.

I combed the fur under my chin and along my neck. I bared my teeth. They looked yellowish, and when I whisked my tongue over them they seemed a little crusty.

I searched about the medicine cabinet and found some toothpaste, a brush, and some mouthwash. A few moments later I felt like one clean and warm and handsome ape.

Seven

Suzie Q had found a pair of blue jeans, and as they were long, she had cuffed the bottoms of the pants legs. She had on a pair of purple tennis shoes and a white tee shirt with a logo that read: MAMA'S SWEET PIES

She looked a little tearful.

"What about Mom and Dad?" she said.

I didn't want to give her false hope, and neither did I want to sound certain, because I was not. But I said, "I think they may have gone down with the ship. And that wouldn't be good."

"But you don't know that."

"I think it is a strong possibility, but I don't know it for sure. We must take care of ourselves. That's what Mom and Dad would have wanted."

She thought for a moment. "Ned is a seal, right?"

"He is."

"Do all seals write on boards?"

"They do not."

"Where are we?"

"We'll call it a craft until we have a better name."

"Is Ned one of the aliens?"

"I don't think so."

She nodded, wiped a tear from her eye, and then straightened up and tried to look strong. She succeeded.

We went out of the room and turned right down the hallway as Ned had instructed.

Eight

The hallway was shiny metal and there were lights along the way, built into the wall in glowing strips. I could hear a slight hum within the walls and there was a sense of movement, though I also got the impression that there was some form of artificial stability at work. The floor seemed to be helping us walk.

When we came to the end of the hall, it emptied into a wide-open room. The room had a clear front, a large window, if you will. There was control panel near the window. I watched the dark water outside of it. Knowing I was way down under in an ocean-going machine gave me the creeps. It beat being out in the water, however, freezing and drowning.

Did the other cruise ships survive?

No idea.

All that seemed clear to me was that there had been a saucer floating in the ocean and the ship Suzie Q and I were on had hit it as surely as if it had been an iceberg, and the ship sank. I had no idea about the other cruise ships. I hadn't seen them for days. They always sailed a slight distance away. I assumed that they continued onward.

In the big room multi-colored lights blinked from a variety of places on the board. There were several swivel chairs placed here and there, fastened to the floor. There was someone sitting in a chair, front and center of the control panel. Ned was nearby at a long table, eating a fish. The fish was on a plate and he was using a fork and knife to eat it. He wasn't using the utensils well, but the fact that he was using them at all was impressive. A thumb and a flipper do not match hands and fingers.

Ned sort of smiled at us. I guess it was a smile. His mouth wrinkled and a few teeth showed. He picked up his pad, which was on the table next to him, used the pencil to write:

YOU LOOK BETTER. YOU SHOULD HAVE SOME FISH.

BUT FIRST, YOU SHOULD MEET SOMEONE.

With that, Ned loudly cleared his throat and the person in the chair in front of the control panel swiveled around. The chair squeaked ever so lightly as he turned to look at us.

Nine

The captain turned out to be nearly hairless, though he had a small amount of sandy hair on his head and a stretch of it under his lip. I was stunned. First, we meet a seal with hot soup, and then we meet a non-ape.

He looked at me without curiosity.

"That's an interesting choice of clothes you two have on," he said.

"You did notice that you and I are a different species?" I said.

It seemed like a reasonable question.

"Me and Ned, sir, have damn near seen it all. On your world evolution went another way. Are there people on your world?"

"We are people," I said. "We are apes that are people."

"I see. So are we, only hairless for the most part. And English speaking, and with a similar history of our own, I wager."

"I'm very confused," I said.

Ned wiped the slate with his flipper, wrote a new message, held it up. SO ARE WE.

"Your line of mammals, no offense, died out," I said. "An evolutionary line that somewhere took a wrong track and didn't make it. We've found fossils, but you're the first I've seen that is more than bones and skulls in photos. I didn't know you existed. Though, I think from looking at you that the archeologists and anthropologists were wrong in thinking you had more hair."

"Logical assumptions," the hairless one said, "considering you are covered in fur, you would think others would be. And I admit to not having one whit of a clue about your archeology. Maybe on your world our kind did die out."

"No maybe," I said.

"Indeed."

"Wait. Your world? I repeat, I am very confused."

"I suggest we eat first," said the near-hairless one. "I imagine your backbones are rubbing your bellies, as my American counterparts say. Fighting the sea and fear and cold can do that to you, can burn an excess of calories."

"We are Americans," I said. "Only we don't say that thing about bellies and backbones. Or, at least, I don't."

"Indeed, you are, but of a different universe and time line. I am English. Quite proud of it, by the way. About that food?"

"We could eat," I said.

Ned held up another message on his slate.

I RECOMMEND THE FISH.

"He always does," said the near hairless one. "Clarence!"

A metallic thing with six spindly cable-like arms and a multitude of long fingers on each of its flat metallic hands glided into the room. It had a pointed head, was maybe six feet tall, and like Ned, was carried about on a sled that didn't touch the floor.

"He's a robot," the hairless one said. "His name is Clarence. He prepares a mean lunch. Shall we start with a bit of cocoa to tide us over, and a spot of explanation for you?"

The near-hairless man asked Clarence to bring us hot cocoa. Clarence instantly made that treat inside of itself. One of his robotic hands had a hole in its finger, and out of that hole came steam, and then hot cocoa, which was shot into cups on a counter.

One by one we received our hot cocoa, brought to us by Clarence, cups in three of its hands.

We found seats and the lights were dimmed slightly, and Ned wrote on his slate.

SETTING THE MOOD TO TELL YOU HOW THINGS ARE MESSED UP.

Near-hairless said, "My name is H. G. Wells, and this young aquatic gentleman is Ned the Seal."

Ned barked like a seal, of course.

"Is there an H. G. Wells on your world, an ape version?"

"Doesn't ring a bell," I said.

"*Time Machine*? It's a book I wrote. Quite popular."

"Sorry, doesn't ring a bell."

"Are you a reader?"

"I am. So is Suzie Q."

"Is there an ape version of Jules Verne?"

"There is," I said. "I've read all of his books."

"Figures," said Wells. "Very well. And what are your names?"

We told him, and then he told us his story, which was part of our story.

The cocoa was good, but very hot. During the explanation, Suzie Q, after finishing her cocoa, fell asleep on the couch.

Ten

It seems that Wells and his friend, Ned the Seal, had other companions. But over time, as they fixed time problems that they had partially created, they were able to get all their friends home, including a giant ape who lived on Mars. Or a version of Mars in another universe. Apparently, there were a lot of universes. It was a little confusing, but there was something about alternate universes, a fish stuck in the controls, a wrong turn at a time tunnel, and so on. I zoned out a little.

"The time problems were much easier to repair than we expected," Wells said. "We found that once we corrected simple things, which meant we had to make sure one thing happened instead of another, everything began to fall into place. Time became right, and all the time lines and world lines that had crossed, sorted themselves. Who would have thought it?"

"What strikes me," I said, "is if you repair time, how do you know what you did makes it all right?"

"We didn't try and mess with the future. We messed with the past to make sure what we knew continued to be true, and our time line. The alternate time lines we knew we had fouled up by doing this and that, were corrected. We wanted the pasts of the alternate worlds to continue to be true to themselves as well. Now the futures will be whatever they make of themselves."

Ned wrote: THAT'S WHAT WE KEEP TELLING OURSELVES.

"Couldn't you have left it as it was, with the mistakes, and lived with it?"

"We knew if certain people won certain wars, or didn't do certain things, we could have a world ruled by fascists. Great inventions and great people might never have come into being. We made sure dogs were developed by breeding. Something we had fouled up, in some way or another. After our original, accidental alteration, no dogs existed in the world we had tampered with, which was our own world. We had to get that right. Who wants to live in a world without dogs? Cats I was less concerned with, but they made it all right on their own, which seems to be a constant with them. Thing is, we worked on the broad strokes and everything fell into place."

Ned held up his tablet.

I THINK SOME THINGS COULD HAVE BEEN BEST SERVED BY CHANGE.

"Our job was to try and leave things as they were."

MESSED UP.

"In some cases, yes."

FISH SEEMED TO TASTE THE SAME EVERYWHERE WE WENT.

"Thank you, Ned," Wells said. "Enlightening. But what caused all this disturbance and brouhaha in the first place was we were pulled across time and space because of something that smelled a lot like a fish..."

Wells paused to look at Ned. Ned looked away.

"—got caught behind the control panel here, and somehow that fishy element lodged in the controls and the wiring in the back. It wasn't the first time. Had to have a special panel put in that I call the fish guard. Anyway, we not only jumped in time, we jumped dimensions. I have since repaired the problem. The time ship works nicely. It flies, moves well under water, along with navigating time, backwards and forwards. But, for reasons unknown, we haven't been able to jump off this alternate world back to our own time line."

FISH HAD NOTHING TO DO WITH IT.

"Yes, Ned," Wells said. "Not this time."

"How long have you been trapped here?" I said.

"A week. By the standards of this world's sunrise and sunset, which we calculated is only slightly shorter than the days on our world. No idea why. Everything looks pretty much the same, so it's a minor mystery."

Ned wrote:

WHO CARES.

"Well, I thank you for rescuing us," I said. "I'm sad to say, I fear we've lost our parents."

"If they were on the ship, I expect so," Wells said.

"Is there any way for us to know? I think I would like to eat, but I think even more I would like to know that."

"We combed the ocean as best we could when the ship went under," Wells said. "We were under water and we saw the lights when the ship first dipped down, and then we rose up. Our sensors told us that someone was standing on our ship. That's when we opened the hatch."

"Is it possible to see the sunken cruise ship?"

"Are you sure you want to do that?"

I nodded.

Wells looked to see that Suzie Q was still asleep.

"Very well, then. Ned, set a course."

Eleven

The little seal moved quickly and confidently, his flippers flapping over the controls as Wells worked at switches and levers. Lights blinked and the ship rolled to the left, but somehow the floor adjusted and we were still standing upright.

We went deep, and soon we were cruising through whipping, wet weeds, and there were fish everywhere, big and small. Ned stood close to the glass, watching them. Soon his nose was pressed to the glass, making little wet smudges. He made a sound that I believe to have been lip smacking.

"Come away from there, Ned," Wells said.

We passed one of the great saucers. It was flat on the ocean floor, like a giant plate turned upside down. There was a wide clear strip of a wind screen that went completely around it. Inside I could see water had found a way in. Alien bodies, spidery looking things with bulbous heads, were floating about. They all appeared connected by long stretches of skin. There were lights inside the saucer. Golden lights and green lights, little silver spots that moved about like fish, floating lights. I thought it might have been the saucer we saw on the surface, the one the ship had collided with. Perhaps it had cruised down close to see the ship, check it out, and had misjudged things, collided with it. The two crafts may have cancelled one another out.

The time machine sailed past the saucer, and in short time, there was the cruise ship.

I had been observing all of this from the couch, but now I left Suzie Q sleeping there, went to stand near the water screen, or window if you prefer, where Ned was whimpering at the fish and still nosing the glass.

The time machine had strong lights and the lights cut through the wet dark, and the ship was like a spear sticking into the ocean bottom, the bow buried deep. The lights from the time machine gathered around it like a halo. Things swirled all about the ship, and as we came closer, I saw those things were items from the ship and passengers. Life vests, clothes and belongings that had once seemed of importance. And then the hairy bodies of my kind floated into our sight. The bodies slow-churned in the water with the fish, like ornaments in an aquarium.

Then a body slammed against the shield. It was none other than Dunderhead. His eyes were open and his mouth was open, and all his clothes had been washed away, or he had been caught naked when the ship went down. His blond fur fluttered around him in the water and the light. A little teddy bear floated near him. There had always been a rumor that he kept a little teddy bear, not too unlike one I had owned when I was a child. I decided that bear was his.

I felt a kind of joy in seeing his corpse hit the shield and bounce away, out of the light and into the deep darkness, but his stuffed bear gave me a feeling of sadness shortly thereafter. He was stupid and pathetic, but in some ways, aren't we all?

Wells circled the great ship. It seemed like a toy now. Bodies were everywhere. There was all manner of unidentifiable objects on the ocean floor.

Though the odds were long, and I never expected it, there they were. My parents.

Floating, holding hands, twisting in the water, their fur lifting from their faces, and finally their bodies flowed away and the time craft passed them by.

I sort of wished I had seen Tomi out there.

I know that's mean, but hey, there it is.

I thought about my parents and burst into tears.

Twelve

Ned was patting my leg with his flipper.

I looked down into his earnest face. His eyes were narrowed. His snout trembled slightly.

I gave his head a pat, went back to the couch, and leaned into it and closed my eyes. I tried not to think of my parents spinning around and around, way down under in the thing I feared most. The depths of the ocean. It was an image that was hard to shake, however. At least they had gone down together, their fingers entwined as if they were one.

Hunger was no longer important to me. The feeling had passed. I tried to think of something pleasant.

I thought of masturbation. I liked that. I thought of sex. I liked that, but, unfortunately, I hadn't had any yet, so masturbation was better to think about. That I knew.

I named my hand Kathy but managed to keep it still inside my clown pants pocket until I drifted into a deep sleep.

Thirteen

It was some hours later when I awoke. I can't honestly be certain of the time, but two or three hours felt right.

We were still cruising under water. Suzie Q was awake and sitting at a table near the control panel, playing chess with Ned. Ned was teaching her how to play by seal-barking and writing notes on his slate.

Suzie Q turned and smiled when she saw me.

"I had a good lunch," she said.

"That's good," I said.

She hadn't seen our parents or Dunderhead, or the horror of the sunken ship. I decided I would tell her later, when the time was right, though I was uncertain exactly when that time would be.

How is there ever a right time for that?

"You should eat," she said.

I thought this was true. I was quite hungry by then. The soup hadn't been very filling and the nap had revived my appetite.

Wells came into the room. No doubt he had heard Suzie Q's words. "Come with me. I'll show you the way to the galley."

I went with him.

It was another large room.

"How big is this craft?" I asked.

"On the outside, it would appear much smaller. But inside, space is warped. It is ten times larger in here than a measurement would make it to be on the outside. We change its shape from time to time. We also have a device that allows languages to be translated so that people who speak different languages can talk to one another and be understood without an awareness that our voices and languages are altered for each other."

"How is that done?"

"I don't know exactly. I invented the original machine. It was stolen by a crazy man, but a brilliant man. He made improvements on the device, including the language decoder, which can be injected into individuals to use when they leave the ship, and I believe he may have stolen alien technology to do it. He became a vampire and fucked Morlocks in the ass."

"What's a Morlock?"

"I wrote about them in a book that has yet to be published but will. I left the ass-fucking out. In a nutshell, they were hairy, mean, and mostly lived underground. It's a long story. The Time Traveler stole the machine. He was not a nice person. He's dead now. I hope. He fell down a great chasm into the earth and disappeared, or so I've been told. But that's another story. Do you know what cabbage is?"

"I do."

"Do you like it?"

"No."

"Good. Because we don't have any. But we do have a lot of other things."

I think that was a joke, but with Wells it was hard to tell.

As for having a lot of different kinds of foods, indeed, they did. There was a massive refrigerator and it was stocked with food.

Wells said, "Pick what you would like."

I made quite a pig of myself. Yes, we have pigs on our world too. Way Wells explained it to me, the only real difference he figured in our world and his is that humans died out and apes were the ones who evolved. He also said that due to what I had said earlier, there didn't appear to be an equivalent to H. G. Wells. That last bit made him sad.

"Ned and I keep improving Time Machine. That's not only what it is, that's also its name. Time Machine. Here's another thing, if you are in this machine and it is moving, you do not age. If it stops, you begin to age at a normal pace. Age doesn't try to catch up. You won't turn older immediately or anything like that. And since Ned and I have been in the machine a lot, we have not aged much, though by our home world time, we have been gone for many years."

The thought of Ned made Wells smile.

"Ned, that little guy, he is so smart. His brain was enhanced by a crazy doctor named Momo. Ned could run this machine by himself. He gets distracted by an overwhelming desire to eat fish, and a certain mischievousness, but other than that, he can handle this device. He can even repair minor problems. We do have a problem neither of us has repaired, however. We're trapped here in this alternate universe. Can't seem to manage a fix, though we have things we plan to try. I think we will figure it out."

"Can you correct what happened to me? You know, go back in time and fix it?"

"No. Yours is an alternate time line not damaged by us. We leave it alone if it wasn't our fault."

"But wouldn't you now be considered part of our time line?"

"Changing that event might save your parents, but the thing is we would not be correcting something, we would be changing it. Not the same thing. I'm sorry, but that isn't how it should work, or will work."

"So, there's no way Suzie Q and I can get our parents back?"

"I'm afraid not. We have already done enough damage in our own time line, and others, and I'm glad we fixed it. But I do not believe it is wise to mess with another time line that, as far as I know, has never been time-damaged. All I know for certain is I want to go home, back to my spot in time, and write more novels. Maybe do a bit of tinkering and experimenting."

"But there are other alternate worlds, correct? Not just yours? I understood that correctly, did I not?"

"That's what I said."

"I know, but I can't keep from asking. It sounds so odd that there is an alternate world to ours, other alternates."

"From our viewpoint, your world is the alternate world. But correct. I meant what I said. There are others. My position is we need to quit messing with time altogether. Go home, raise families, write books, create inventions, whatever it was we were planning to do originally."

"When you do go back, what happens to Ned?"

"I suppose that is up to Ned."

"What happens to us?"

"I suppose that is up to the two of you."

Fourteen

It was hard to do, but I told Suzie Q that our parents were dead. I didn't give her the details, the awful thing I had seen, them spinning about in the water, around and around. I thought it was best not to, but I did explain to her that I knew they were dead. Later, when she was older, I would tell her that their fingers were entwined. But right now, that wouldn't help her feel any better. It was best to tell her they were dead and not provide details.

I also explained that we could stay in our world, or go where Ned and Wells went, provided they found a way to leave where they were now stranded. We could go with them, if they managed to get the craft to jump world and dimension, but if we were to go to their world, we would look too out of place. Wells had explained it to me, and he was right. On his world, we would have been freaks. Yet, there was nothing for us on our own world. It had changed too much, and the things that mattered most to us, our parents, were dead.

"But, what about Ned?" Suzie Q asked. "Wouldn't he be thought a freak?"

"Too cute," I said. "He might not like the idea, but Wells said it was his belief that Ned could get by as an exotic pet, if he didn't write on his slate. I don't know. He also said Ned might end up somewhere else as well, some place where he needn't hide his artificially enhanced intelligence. I doubt he would like to be a pet."

I thought of our own world, of course. We were already there, but home had disease and aliens, and even though we were inoculated, it would be a lonely and dangerous place.

One bright spot. Wells said he and Ned had seen many saucers falling from the skies, and he suggested that though they had dropped a disease on us, that perhaps some simple bacteria from our world had not agreed with them. He said he was going to write a book about just that. He thought that if they had died of disease, after releasing disease, it would be ironic. He said he knew of whole cultures that had been wiped out, or nearly wiped out, by disease, so it made sense.

Still, our home world did not sound like a place I wanted us to be. Strangely, at that moment, I felt more at home in Time Machine than anywhere else. I found the presence of Ned and Wells comforting, and so did Suzie Q. For the moment, it was impossible to think of being anywhere else. I also thought Clarence made dandy hot chocolate.

The next few days went pleasantly by. Wells and Ned worked on problems with the machine, and at some point, they figured out how to repair it. They were quite jovial about it.

Ned spun his sled around and around, which of course spun him around and around. He nearly always smelled of fish and the spinning of the sled wafted the odor throughout the craft.

I nearly passed out from tuna smell.

Fifteen

The world Suzie Q and I knew was to be left behind, like pocket lint in discarded pants. We were done with it. We were about to jump to another time line. It wouldn't be our final destination, as Wells pledged to help us find a place that suited us and would not call attention to our appearance. In the meantime, he said we would be on holiday, and he and Ned would be our hosts.

In the control room, we strapped into our chairs, and Wells and Ned pushed buttons and pulled levers and turned knobs, then pushed one big blue button, and we rose out of the ocean.

The water sloshed over the view shield as we were lifted, and then Time Machine splashed completely clear and the sun was bright and yellow like a busted egg yolk. The water appeared white for a long moment as our eyes adjusted to the brightness, and then it was blue.

We could see in the distance a stretch of land, and there was a huge cloud rising from it. Or rather there was a long puffy tunnel that stretched from the ocean and went high in the sky. At the top of the funnel was a greater cloud that was roiling dramatically. The water rippled in the distance, all the way to the shore, and then the sea elevated into a massive wave and charged toward us. All the ocean was an expanding, moving wall of water, with what appeared to be a peak of dark ash. Time Machine shook.

"They went and did it," Wells said. "Turned against each other. They didn't need the aliens to destroy them. They did it themselves."

And then, ahead of the massive ash-tipped wave, Time Machine jumped.

Sixteen

Jumping is a bit unpleasant at first, akin to sea sickness, but not as long lasting. The large window we looked out of glowed orange-hot, or at least it looked hot, though I admit to feeling nothing different in my seat. I was comfortable. A little scared and a lot confused, but comfortable.

The window, or view shield, stayed orange for a time, and then a lot of colors came along and changed orange to blue to red to green, and you could hear Time Machine hum like a drunk trying to remember a tune. Away we went down a tunnel of white with dark swirls at the side.

It was then that I began to see things in the swirls. Images, flashes, and then one of the saucers appeared in front of us, and there were bodies from the ship (thank goodness, I did not see our parents among them) and Wells deftly whipped the machine around them.

As he did there was a flash of light, and I was temporarily blind. When I could see, everything was blue, and darker blue in spots where there were tunnels shooting off in all directions. And then the tunnels became fewer, and there were two, not counting the straight path we were on. One went left and one went right. We veered left. The tunnel seemed to grab at us, sucking us along at high speed. It was as if we were in the belly of a python. Time Machine made a droning noise and there was another flash of white light, and then we were blind again.

When we could see once more the view shield was dark and the lights in Time Machine were a soft yellow, like being inside an egg yolk.

Ned rode over on his sled, scribbled on his pad, held it up for us to see.

WHERE DO YOU WANT TO GO?
I looked at Suzie Q. She shrugged.
"We have no place to go. Ned, you pick."
He scribbled on his pad.
I LIKE HAWAII.
We jumped again.

Seventeen

"This is not Polynesia before Captain Crook," Wells said.

"What now?" I said.

"Ned here has made an error. He was supposed to set the controls for Polynesia at a time when it was free from outside influence. He thought it might be a nice place to vacation and possibly live. For the two of you, and for himself. I know how he thinks. It turns out there are holes in the holes of time. He forgot to anticipate this, which has happened before."

Ned raised a flipper as if he needed to identify himself, then held up his slate.

I PICKED. SET THE DESTINATION. YOU WORKED THE CONTROLS.

"So, it's like that, is it?" Wells said.

Ned wrote again. DAMN TOOTIN'

"Beside the point," Wells said. "There are holes in the holes, and that's the problem. There were peculiarities in the jump."

Ned held up the slate again after a furious burst of writing.

I DID MY JOB.

"Ned," Wells said, "we both did. I suppose it's no one's fault."

Ned wiped the slate with his flipper, wrote again.

IT MIGHT BE YOURS A LITTLE.

"No one's fault."

YOU SET THE JUMP CONTROLS.

"That will do, Ned."

IF YOU SAY SO.

I looked out the window, which is a much easier term than windshield or view glass, or what have you. The world below was white. It was covered in ice. It certainly was not Polynesia as we knew it on our world, or Polynesia of our past. We had that place on our earth. A lot of exotic apes lived there. They wore flowers around their necks. After talking with Wells, I understood that we had a similar history with our islands. Our captain who "discovered" it all and led to inhabitation by Europeans was not named Cook, however. He was called Crook. Lots of similarities in our worlds. A few differences.

Red lights blinked on the console.

Ned wrote on his slate.

UH OH.

———◆———

There were problems with Time Machine.

Wells landed it gently on the ice. He and Ned spent time looking at the controls, opening the back of the control panel. Wrenches were wrenched, screwdrivers were screwed. Small hammers hammered.

When the two of them came out from behind the control panel, Wells said, "The problem seems elsewhere." He turned to Ned. "I better not find a fish stuffed somewhere where it shouldn't be."

Ned started to write on his slate, then paused and let the slate drop back against him along with the marker which was fastened about his neck on a chain.

"It's a rare situation, but the outside panel has to be investigated. I think something has burned out." Wells said.

"Can it be fixed?"

"I believe it can, but it will take time to recharge. Maybe a day or two, if that is in fact the problem. We need to open the outside panel, remove the charge jumper and the refibulator, and replace them. It's a little thing, and easy to fix, but then the trouble is the time it takes for the whole thing to recharge using solar energy and the time essence. Something it can locate and absorb."

"There's a time essence?" I said.

"It's what allows us to travel through time."

Ned held up his slate.

HE DOESN'T REALLY KNOW HOW ANY OF THIS WORKS.

"Ha, ha," Wells said.

Eighteen

They gave me and Suzie Q hooded coats, and put on coats themselves, even Ned, though his was a slip-over that gave room for his head and flippers. He wore his slate on the outside of his coat, his marker dangling beside it.

We went through a door that spun open as if it were water fleeing down a drain, and once we were outside, it closed the same way behind us.

It was cold out there, and I do mean cold. When we breathed there were clouds of frost. Ned scooted over the ice on his sled.

After a bit, Ned stopped and wrote on his slate.

MY ASS IS COLD.

"He has grown soft," Wells said.

I GOT YOUR SOFT, Ned wrote.

"He talks about adventure more than he does it these days. He likes the inside of Time Machine too much."

Right then, I was thinking I liked the inside of it as well.

We went along for a time, and then we were astonished to see greenery appear. Bushes first, and then there were slightly larger and stouter trees, and finally a forest. We realized we were very gradually descending. And then things changed, and the descent was more obvious. We could see an enormous gap in the ground. It was not a drop-off, but a large hole that slanted down, as if we were on the sides of a coffee saucer. Warm air was coming up from the hole. It felt good.

It was an easy enough descent for a while. We went down into the warmth, and soon I was sweating. I threw my hood back, as did the others, and eventually we came to a valley.

We could see it below us and there was a river winding through it. There were great trees, the biggest I had ever seen, and they were rising into brightness, which was confusing, considering where we were, down low in the world. The great trees had a split between them that I judged to be a half mile wide, but keep in mind we were high up and looking down, and I'm not a great judge of distance.

"This is most peculiar," said Wells. "I suggest we go back to Time Machine and investigate with its aid."

It was a long trek back. It was cold and dark when we got there. Once inside, we removed our coats and strapped in. The ship couldn't make a time jump yet, as it had to recharge, or whatever it did, but it could fly, and Wells and Ned lifted us up and guided us through the darkness with the ship's great lights. We sailed like a kite on a high wind. Down we went into the hole and into the warm, green valley.

As we went down, it turned bright, and it being night and us going down into the earth, that didn't make any sense.

Then again, the last few weeks, with the saucers, the cruise ships, our rescue by Time Machine, which contained a writer-inventor and a highly intelligent seal, didn't make a lot of sense either.

Nineteen

We cruised over the high trees and down into a treeless part of the valley, hovered at the place where the trees split. Through the window we could see a vast field of waving yellow and green grass. There were monstrous trees on all sides of the field. In the trees were magnificent blooms of all colors. And then the blooms moved, lifted to flight, and I realized that what I was seeing in the bright light was the heads of colorful birds, not blooms.

Considering how far away they were, and how large they looked taking to the air, they were most likely far larger than they appeared, which would make them some big-ass birds.

Wells expertly set the craft down in the field of waving grass, and for a long moment we maintained our seats and looked at the grass swaying. Eventually, the spell broke, and we got up and put on our coats and went through the swirling door and out into the grass.

There was a sun above us. It was the color of a fresh egg yolk full of bloody chick, but it wasn't the sun we knew. It seemed closer to the earth and smaller, yet it was quite comfortable. The red in its yellow swirled as if stirred. The clouds were thin and those that blew in front of the sun turned transparent. The grass was nearly to our waists, and it was moving gently against us. It gave off a sweet smell, somewhat like lavender, but not quite. The tassel on Ned's fez whipped about.

Behind us we could see how at the end of the gap it slanted up, and up, and up, and there was great darkness there. The night of the upper world was oozing in. That was the path we had used to come down into this world of golden light. We could feel a light cold wind from that direction, blowing down the long slanting funnel from above.

"This is a world within a world, as Verne wrote about," Wells said. "We are inside the earth, at least somewhat. And this sun, it makes no sense."

Ned wrote on his slate.

IT'S VOLCANIC IN ORIGIN.

"Perhaps," Wells said.

PERHAPS MY ASS.

"You can't know for sure, Ned."

I'M A GOOD GUESSER.

"Have it your way."

YOU MEAN THE RIGHT WAY.

"He is cute, but he can be insufferable," Wells said.

I AM CUTE.

We stood in the field and talked for a while. It was mostly chatter. We were excited to have discovered there was a world inside of a world. Above it was a place of ice and snow, and down below, a golden sun and gigantic trees and swaying grass.

The machine couldn't jump time, but it could still move, but even that would soon end, Wells said, as the recharging that it needed would take quite a while, or so he estimated after he had a look at the damage. He was uncertain how well the sun above would charge the device, and therefore his estimate of the time needed was uncertain. The device that required charging turned out to be about the size of a locket and was on a chain.

"There used to be two solar chargers, but one—"

And here Wells paused to look long and hard at Ned.

"—was lost."

Ned wrote rapidly.

IT WAS AN ACCIDENT.

"So, we're standing next to a great flow of mud, and I ask Ned if the charger is safe, and he said, 'Yes', on his pad, of course, and then he takes the charger from around his neck and begins to swing it on its chain to prove he has it and it's safe, and I say, 'Ned, do not do that. The chain might break'. He shook his head and kept swinging it, faster and faster. And then guess what?"

"The chain broke?" Suzie Q said.

"Exactly, and away went that beautiful shiny blue charger into the great pit of boiling mud, and volcanic activity—"

LIKE THE SUN ABOVE US.

Ned finished writing that after Wells had moved on, but he held it up and wriggled around like a kid, flashing his slate.

"—and that was the end of that. Now we only have one charger, which is all you need, but another would speed the process, and they are very hard to create. For one thing, you either need an actual diamond or a very large piece of clear quartz to construct one."

Ned clutched a chain around his neck with a flipper and a thumb. It was a different chain from the one that held his slate and pencil. He pulled from inside his coat a diamond-shaped pendant, blue in color. The diamond was in the center of it. It was not blue, but the pulsing light of the pendant made it seem blue. He took the chain from around his neck and held it with flipper and thumb.

Wells glared at him.

"Ned, you're not supposed to bring that out again. If it comes out, I'm supposed to carry it to avoid an accident, which you must admit you were responsible for the time before."

Ned began to swing the chain and pendant above his head, around and around, looking directly at Wells while he did it, his mouth curled, a few teeth showing.

"Ned," Wells said, "please don't do that."

Ned sneered.

The chain broke.

The pendant flew way out into the high grass and disappeared amongst the waving strands.

We all looked at Ned.

The snide grin disappeared. He wrote on his pad.

WELL, SHIT.

Twenty

The good news is the tall grass was not the same as boiling mud, and we found the device. I came across it and gave it to Wells. I had to agree with Wells about Ned when it came to the pendant. He was not responsible enough.

Ned had gone about the motions of helping us look for the device, but he mostly cruised around on his sled and looked pouty. He wrote something about how the chain was supposed to be stronger than the one before. This didn't prove to be the case, obviously, and was beside the point.

Still, even though we found the pendant, it took us a long time to do so. The grass was thick and had to be carefully searched.

By the time we found it, I would have thought the sun would have moved, but it had not. It remained central and it was no warmer or cooler than before, except when the wind came, and it came from the direction of the gap. Arctic air mixed with interior sun. When the wind blew hard, and from time to time it did, it could be almost unpleasant, as cool and damp as it was.

We climbed back into the machine, and a cloaking device was activated. A few buttons were punched and the machine was made invisible from the outside. The charger, which was now in Wells's pocket, absorbed the heat of the sun. It didn't have to be directly exposed to the sun, but it had to be outside to take in and contain the energy of light. It could be fastened to the inside of the wind-shield of Time Machine, but the problem was the cloaking device muted the amount of sunlight it could absorb, and therefore it took longer to charge.

Wells's idea was to rest, and accept we were going to be here for a while until the device charged. After we ourselves were recharged, we would search for a safe place to reposition the device, and while we rested, we would hang the amulet inside, and when we went out, we would take it with us, as it could charge even while in a pocket.

I wanted to explore, not only to satisfy curiosity, but also because I thought less about my parents when I was busy.

Eager as we all were, Wells insisted on rest first. Ned held up his slate. It read: WELLS IS GETTING OLD.

We rested, though I didn't truly relax all that much, anticipating our exploration to come. I lay in my bed trying to read a book from one of many in the shelves. Thackeray's *Vanity Fair*. I couldn't decide if my inability to read it was my lack of taste, my excitement, or that the book stunk.

I know I was relieved when we were set free to explore in our lighter clothes, without the hot bundle of coats. By this point, Suzie Q and I had abandoned the clown outfits and had discovered in other rooms more normal-looking clothes that fit.

Out on the grassy field we decided to walk toward the trees on the far side of the gap. It was a long walk. We had brought food from inside the machine. We laid out a blanket and put our basket of food on it, then we all sat down for a picnic where the grass faded out, right before the forest began again on the far side. Wells had replaced the chain on the charger and had hung it around his neck. I saw Ned eyeing it from time to time.

It was an amazing thing, having a picnic inside the earth. I don't know how far we were down. Certainly, this wasn't the center of the earth, but it was without question a world inside of a world, and it was fascinating.

We sat and ate, and while we were eating, we saw all those great birds again, the ones that had heads that were white or red or blue, the occasional green or glossy black. It was a beautiful sight, all those colors moving across the sky, glistened by the sun. They were closer to us this time, and indeed, they were large. The largest birds I have ever seen. They could have placed a condor in their pockets, if they had had any.

As we finished eating, we saw that the squadron of birds were still moving above us, and swiftly. Their great shadows ran over us and darkened the earth. Through a natural path that cut its way through the trees, we could see some of them still, and they were starting to dip down to earth.

"That is most interesting," Wells said.

Ned wrote on his slate.

HOW DO YOU KNOW WHAT IS INTERESTING ABOUT BIRDS?

Wells ignored him.

I must say, Ned was being quite the pill. He was still angry that he had lost the amulet while showing off.

"Shall we have a short look?" Wells said. "I'm curious to know where they are gathering."

Ned held up his slate.

TREES. THEY ARE GATHERING IN TREES.

"You don't know that," said Wells.

THEY'RE BIRDS.

"Let's go into the woods a way and take a look," Wells said. "If we don't come across them in a reasonable time, we'll start back. The amulet has to charge, so we should be outside for a while anyway. What say the rest of you?"

"Let's explore," Suzie Q said, and I nodded in agreement.

Ned still looked pouty. But he wrote:

I GUESS THAT'S ALL RIGHT.

We folded up our blanket and left the basket, as the food was gone now anyway, with plans to pick it up on our way back to the machine.

As we went along in the woods, the trail grew clearer due to the closeness of the trees. The shadows from the trunks and limbs cut out much of the sunlight and didn't allow things to grow on the ground, made it so it was like walking through a park.

This caused our trip to be shady and cool, but it didn't help us in the amulet department, the sun being less present. Wells said as much, and we were about to start back, when Ned pointed a flipper skyward toward a gap in the trees.

The birds were circling and the circle they made was thick with color and feathers. The made loud cawing noises, and the noises were frantic, and finally the birds began to lower themselves and then they disappeared behind the trees. Dark smoke was rising there as well. It drifted over the trees and against the bright sky.

We didn't discuss it, but we began following in the direction the birds had gone. Before us the trees were thinning. There was sunlight there, and it was thick and warm looking. We eased into the opening and saw why the birds were descending.

The answer was quite unexpected.

Twenty-one

There were no trees in the spot we came to. There were stumps that had been set afire and were smoking gently in the cool wind. In the middle was a huge mound of hardened mud. It rose forty feet high and was quite wide, and there were steps cut into the dried mud that led to a flat top. The birds were landing there in a swarm. There was smoke up there too, dark smoke. The smoke drifted between the fluttering birds and clouded the clear sky, and the sunlight that came through it was streaked with shadows made by the smoke where it was thickest.

The birds were very excited. They cawed loudly, and there were other sounds, and they were so unexpected we didn't realize they were screams until they had gone on a while.

Wells grabbed a limb that had fallen on the ground and began to rush toward the mound. Behind him Ned jetted along on his sled. I fetched a limb as well and told Suzie Q to head back into the woods and to remain there. She hesitated only for a moment before rushing into the concealment of the forest.

Up the mound Wells went, bounding up the steps. Ned's sled glided up them a bit at a time, tilting precariously, threatening to throw the seal out of the machine and turn him into a bouncing bundle on the hard mud steps. But by the time I was halfway up, both Ned and Wells had made the top.

I heard Wells yelling and there was a savage flutter of wings and screeches. The birds went up and circled and continued to screech. They swooped down from time to time, then flew back up at enormous speed. I viewed all of this through smoke and strips of sunlight.

On top of the mound I saw Wells swinging his stick at the birds, and some of them acted as if to fight him, but after he caught one or

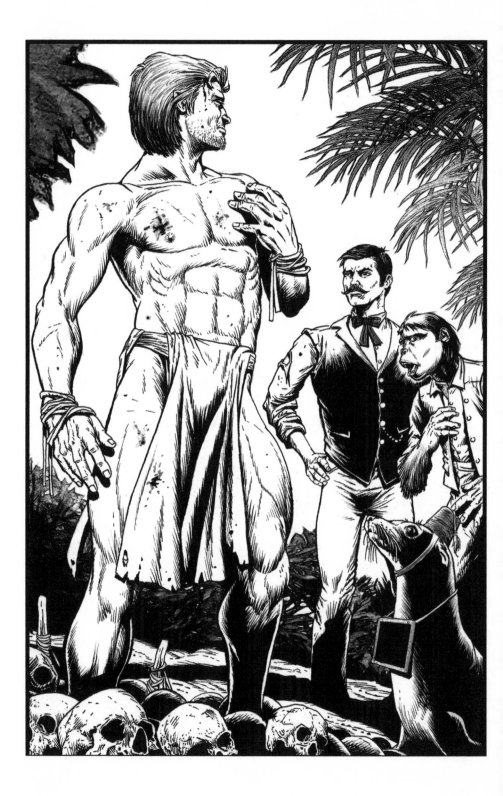

two upside the head, hitting one hard enough it fell to the ground and quivered, I saw what all the commotion was about.

There were fragments of corpses that had been picked over by the birds. Some of the fragments were on fire and others smoked from having been. One man with his entrails dangling was screaming, but that ended not long after I reached the summit of the mound. His life had finally drained.

I could see in the middle of the mound another man. He was large, not an ape. He had thick wadded blond hair and tanned skin. He wore only a leather loin cloth. He was large and muscular. His hands and feet were bound to the mud by pegs and thick ropes. One of the ropes had broken loose from the peg that bound his right arm. The way he had been staked out was crucifixion style. With the loose hand he had one of the birds by the throat and was leaning into it, biting its neck. The bird's wings beat wildly as blood squirted on the man's face and torso.

The other birds continued to swoop down. Now I too was swinging my stick. The birds would come in and snap their beaks at me. One of them bit me on the shoulder. I didn't realize at first that I had been bitten, but then the blood came. It ran warm under my clothes and then the pain came. I fought on, trying to ignore it.

Ned, sitting on his sled, had a long rod in his hand. It had to have been stored on the sled, because I had not seen it before. He was pointing it at the birds when they came near. Out of its tip came wavering strands of electric blue fire that hit the birds and made them shriek and smoke and take back to the sky. Brightly colored feathers were all over the place, as well as drifting down from the heavens.

And then it was over.

The birds gathered together in a flock of color, wheeled as if a whistle had been blown in command, and began to fly away.

It was a good thing. I was worn thin from swinging that stick, and I was bleeding profusely. Still, I felt good. I had managed to live through another life-threatening event, and I felt a little heroic. I had never felt brave or heroic in my whole life. This is the moment when I truly felt I had changed. I could have run away, and I had not. Actually, I had charged into action.

I looked at the tied man. Saw him breaking the rope on his bound arm, so that now both arms were free. He bent forward to work at the ties that bound his feet. By that time, Wells was there and had produced a pocket knife and was sawing at the bonds that bound the big man's ankles.

A moment later the man stood up. He was very tall. He stood well above Wells. My guess was he was six feet and four inches tall. His shaggy blond hair was parted in the middle. It touched his shoulders. He appeared to be all muscle.

Now that I was close I could see his bronze body was covered in thin white scars. There were also some red open wounds, and some of those were crusted with scab, some were open and raw. He had hard features, but I think humans like Wells would probably have thought of him as handsome. I had seen a lot of photos in books while on Time Machine, old Greek statues, quite unlike those I had known on earth. Their representations of the gods were hairless for the most part, though there was usually hair on their heads and sometimes their faces. This man had a dark blond swath across his face that was a mixture of beard (beards being something I had learned about) and dark charcoal stains from burning wood and puffing smoke.

He looked at us and smiled some fine slightly blood-stained teeth, said, "How do you do? Let me thank you for your assistance and introduce myself. Most people call me Jack. Some call me Tango, like the dance."

Twenty-two

"**D**amn, man, what the hell is going on here?" Wells said.

"I suggest we move to a more secure place," Jack said.

"I can recommend one," Wells said.

Ned wrote and held up his slate.

HOLY SHIT. IT'S LORD BLOOMINGDALE, ALSO KNOWN AS TANGO THE MONKEY MAN.

Wells studied Ned's slate, then turned back to Jack.

"He's right," Jack said. "I am indeed Lord Jack Bloomingdale, known as Tango, but you can drop the monkey man part. I was raised by apes, very humanoid apes, not unlike him."

He pointed at me.

"I'm on a quest, but right now I would appreciate food and a place to rest comfortably for a short time. I need to arm myself and go about attempting a rescue, though so far, I've failed dramatically in that department. Which is why you have found me here, tied down on the Hill of Blood and Bones. Clever name, don't you think?"

"It's called that?" I said.

"No. I made that up. Well, I guess it can be called that now, can't it?"

The words seemed strange coming out of the big man's mouth. He was such a wild-looking specimen, one would have expected him to grunt and growl and fling his own dung, instead of speaking calmly and clearly.

Ned held up his slate again.

I READ ABOUT YOU IN MAGAZINES.

"Don't believe everything you read," Jack said. "It was far more exciting."

Ned cleared his slate with the back of his flipper, wrote again.

I HAVE SEEN YOUR PHOTO IN THE PAPERS.

"I don't actually photograph well," Jack said. "I think I'm far more interesting looking and handsome in person, don't you?"

Ned wrote again.

AGREED.

I couldn't decide if Jack was conceited or just extremely confident. Maybe it was his way of joking.

We started back into the forest. Suzie Q came out of the shadows of the trees.

Jack said, "More of you. As I said, I'm quite acquainted with apes. Though I do say you appear to be more advanced than my ape family. It's in your carriage, the way you hold your head. Human-like."

"We call ourselves human on our world," I said.

"Your world? Ah? Time travel, alternate universes, or do we mean extraterrestrial?"

"I think a little of one and two and none of three," I said.

"By the way," Jack said as we walked. "There are groups who translate themselves as humans, but the more civilized they are, the less human they are. At least those that were trying to kill me, the birds, they were honest in their intent.

"The others who put me on the mound, they are men like the poor bastards who died up there. Normally I would have handled them quite well and would have escaped. But there were too many of them and I was tired, and in a rare situation, due to my exhaustion, I was taken by surprise. I was crossing their land unannounced, but they could have been more hospitable. Of course, I did kill a few of them defending myself. Perhaps more than a few."

"The others on the mound?" Wells asked.

"Not sure. They were already there when I arrived. Competitors for resources is my guess. That one poor wretch you must have heard screaming, the birds worked on him for a long time. I was able to get an arm free and defend myself. But in the end, I might not have escaped in time. Thank you again."

Twenty-three

Inside the machine, Ned showed Jack where to shower, and while we waited on him to finish, Wells found medical supplies and food for him.

Jack went about his business quickly and presented himself to us with damp hair and a shaved face, which I really didn't like as well. He was wearing a white bathrobe which stood out in stark contrast against his tanned skin. He carried his loin cloth in his hand.

"Now, if I could have that medical attention, and some food. I need to rest briefly and be on my way. I don't suppose you have a spear or a bow and arrow, or for that matter just a good knife? The tribesmen, for lack of a better name, took the weapons I had from me. Very heathen of them."

BUT AREN'T YOU A HEATHEN?

Ned held this up on his slate and revealed his teeth. I thought he might be smiling. So, did Jack. Jack let out a laugh.

"I suppose I am. I'm a sophisticated heathen. But no doubt, I feel far more at home in the jungle than in a palace, though I do cut a mean rug at dance functions. I'm assuming from this machine that you are from the future."

"Different dimensional world, but related to this one," Wells said.

"Makes sense," Jack said.

"You seem quite calm about it all," I said.

"I've been around and I've seen a few things. More than a few. I'm also blessed with a longevity drug. Considering I'm good-looking and have money, gold and jewels from back home, you'd have to say I've been blessed, wouldn't you?"

"I suppose so," Wells said. "And modest as well."

"An important trait, I think," Jack said. "Without modesty, you only have ego. I mean, if it's true, then I'm not being immodest. Am I correct?"

"Indeed," Wells said.

Jack ate, but when it came to weapons, outside of Ned's electric stunner, no weapons of the sort he requested were on board, except a big butcher knife.

Jack balanced the butcher knife in his hand. "I'll fashion a guard for it. Otherwise your hand slips over the blade when it becomes wet with blood. I can make one easily enough with some carved wood and resin. Quite sufficient to start with. Perhaps I can make a bow and arrows if time and situation permit. Or simple spears, essentially sharpened sticks, and I can fire-harden the tips."

"So how did you end up bound on top of a mound of dried mud with birds trying to eat you, along with those other poor chaps?" Wells said.

Jack peeled the robe off his shoulders so that Wells could attend to his wounds with ointment and a grease of some sort.

"Let me merely say it was an error in judgment. I think I gave you the bulk of it. I was trespassing. Tired. There were a lot of them. If you will allow me some food, I need to return to my mission."

"I would fly you there," Wells said. "The machine can do a bit of that. I mean, there's still juice left to operate the insides here, to go short distances. But we have to be careful not to run all the juice out. Do that, it takes ten times longer to recharge, now that we only have one device to make that possible."

Wells gave Ned a glance. Ned was suddenly busy adjusting something on his sled.

"I wouldn't ask that," Jack said. "Besides where I need to go, the route might change according to circumstances. Some supplies would be enough."

Wells was wrapping a white bandage around Jack's body, covering one of the largest of the doctored wounds as they spoke.

"Of course," Wells said. "But won't you tell us what your mission is. I don't need to know, but I admit, curiosity has the better of me."

"The Golden Fleece," Jack said.

"Say what?" Wells said.

"The Golden Fleece," Jack said again.

Wells looked at me. I could understand what he was about to ask before he did. I told him that we indeed had the same myth.

"How can there be a real fleece?" Wells said. "It's a myth."

"Perhaps in your world, and to be clear, it is somewhat of a myth topside and downside here. Or to be more precise, a myth has grown up about it. It exists, and is in fact the fleece of a golden ram-like creature. A visitor from the stars. Walked on hind feet, had horns, the whole nine yards."

"I only thought I had seen everything," Wells said.

"We never see it all," Jack said. "But some of us have seen more than others. But, as we humans do, we misunderstood the benevolent presence of the aliens who could heal with a touch, and so we killed them all. One escaped to here, but over time, he, she, it, whatever the proper designation is, died. The place where he lived in this down-deep world was free of sickness of any kind. He was possessed of an inert ability to live forever, as am I. Something fell on him and killed him. A rotting, but heavy limb, is what I've heard. Otherwise he would still be alive. When the alien died, he was skinned and the fleece, for his wool was thick and golden, was hung on a great limb, and a shrine was built around it. Anyone who might be sick goes there, and they are instantly healed when the fleece is draped over them."

"And if you believe that, I'd like to sell you a dancing pig who flies on Tuesdays," Wells said.

Jack laughed. "I know how you feel, but it's true. I remember the aliens. I remember how humans reacted. Along with others, nine others, I tried to prevent the wholesale slaughter of these powerful and benevolent aliens who were very poor at defending themselves. But there was a great tide of anti-otherness blowing over the earth. It was so powerful it was like a dark wind out of nowhere. Reason was not a part of it. Anything different from humans, as they were perceived on the above world, was considered evil. It made no difference that they did not attack and only brought blessings, it would only do to have them killed, and then destroyed. Their ships and bodies were burned. Those who touched them found themselves to be in excellent health, and they ceased to age. But it was too late for the rest of mankind. We had destroyed the golden goose, or, in this case, the golden rams and ewes that could have given health and permanence to all mankind. The aliens were powerful and could heal, but they could die by accident and murder, and did. The last one found this place, this Down World, came here to hide, but he picked the wrong tree to be under, or so the story goes. I admit, I never saw this particular alien, and know of him only through legend."

"Typical," Wells said. "Our friends here, the hairy ones, had a similar experience on their world."

"Yep," I said.

"My darling Jill and I have lived here for many upper earth years. The concrete growth up there, the short-sided thinking and hatred, led us here to live wild and free, the way I had grown up when the world upstairs was brighter and finer. I was a vagabond in the jungle, left there due to a plane crash, raised by apes, but it was an honest way to live. Assholes were obvious, and they didn't hide behind politics, a piece of paper and a fountain pen. Well, I suppose fountain pens are a thing of the past, but you get my meaning. My old world is gone, and though here can be a world of terror, I prefer it to the one upstairs, what it has become. I brought much of my gold and jewels here, or had it brought. Even down here it has worth. So, I am well situated. Jill and I could have lived here as long as neither murder or accident or war came to us, but then Jill became ill. As for the fleece, it is housed in a distant land, and that is where I am headed, to steal it."

"Steal it?" I said.

"After all my noble words, I must become less noble. My Jill is ill. It's a lingering disease. A sleeping disease. She is slowly dying. It could take a year if one could measure years here. I go by my inner clock. Jill sleeps in a big white room with doctors in white, all paid for by me, folks from upstairs who may find what they've been paid worthless if they return to the surface. It's going to hell fast up there. I left a number of my companions with Jill to watch over her and make sure she receives food in liquid form, fed to her through a tube, her ass wiped for her, her bed clothes and sleeping garments changed, kept clean. In time, she will die if I fail in my quest. She may have died already. I have been gone a long time on this quest. But I still am determined to complete my mission."

I would never have thought Jack to be a talker, being all savage-like in appearance, but I was discovering that when he wanted to talk, you couldn't shut him up. I wasn't sure I saw a lot of difference in topside and down-deep. They were both savage, and the definition as to why didn't matter. They were humans, as we were humans with fur, and as far as I could tell, we didn't learn a thing from history or experience, fur or not. But then, I am eighteen, so what could I possibly know?

"After I have used the fleece to save Jilly, I will return it," Jack said. "If it will not be loaned to me, I will take it, and do whatever is necessary to have it. Jilly means everything to me, and I won't be stopped in my course, no matter the consequences."

"That sounds like true love," I said.

"Yes, it is. When you have lived as long as Jill and I, however, you define it differently. We are not bound by legality alone, though we were married officially and by a priest. A religion neither of us believed. It seemed like the right choice at the time. We are faithful to one another, but we are not monogamous. When you look as we do, and when you don't age, some situations require a different viewpoint."

"Are you speaking of free love?" Wells said. "I believe in that, myself."

"Love is never free, my friend."

When Jack's wounds were dressed, Wells and Ned put together some dried meats and vegetables and fruit, as they would be light to carry, and gave Jack a few metal containers of sardines (which I could tell Ned was loath to part with), as well as a canteen of water. The food was in a pack that Jack could wear on his back.

While this was prepared, Jack rid himself of the robe and put his loin cloth on again. He did this right in front of us. I was too modest for that sort of thing, and was amazed he was not, but him doing it seemed perfectly natural. It certainly intrigued Suzie Q, though I hasten to add, there was nothing sexual or voyeuristic intended on Jack's part. Jack needed to change, and he did. But damn, that was some dick.

Jack napped for a couple of hours in a back room, then used some wood from the wood shop and made himself a guard for the butcher knife using tools from the tool kit there. He did not have to resort to resin, as Wells had some powerful glue on hand. Jack was quite a craftsman and was able to make the guard for the butcher knife in less than a couple of hours, as well as sharpen the blade to a fine edge.

Jack made himself a scabbard for the knife from a spare belt and a tarpaulin. I watched him do this work, and when he was finished, he headed into the kitchen and had a large chunk of meat and drank deeply from a container of water and prepared to set out. I was astonished at how fresh he seemed. His recovery powers were astonishing.

I looked over and saw that Ned had a pack on his sled, as well as his stun gun and two canteens of water.

He had written on his slate:

I'M GOING TOO.

"Oh, Ned, no," Wells said.

IT WILL TAKE A LONG TIME TO CHARGE THE MACHINE. I MAY BE BACK BEFORE YOU LEAVE.

He wiped the slate clean, wrote:

IF YOU CAN'T WAIT OR COME BACK FOR ME, SO BE IT. I DON'T THINK I CAN GO BACK TO A LIFE OF HANGING OUT ON ROCKS, SWIMMING, AND GETTING SEAL NOOKIE AND EATING FISH.

He wiped the board again.

I WOULD, OF COURSE, MISS FISH. AND SEAL NOOKIE. MOSTLY FISH.

"My path is a difficult one, brave little seal," Jack said.

I AM A SEAL THAT HAS HAD MUCH ADVENTURE. TELL HIM, WELLS.

"He has had much adventure," Wells said. "But Ned, you're safe here. Stay with us. You've grown lazy, you know that you're better off here."

Ned shook his head and held out his flipper.

Slowly, Wells took it and shook it.

"Good luck, Ned."

Ned nodded.

"I'm going as well," I said.

"And me too," Suzie Q said. "I can make and shoot a bow and arrow. And I'm very good at it. I won some school championships. They said I could go to the Olympics. Tell them, Bill."

"This is true," I said.

Jack smiled at Suzie Q. "That is impressive. But, I move quickly," he said. "You won't be able to keep up with me."

Ned spun his sled around and around, then raced around the room, and came to an abrupt stop in front of Jack.

"Okay," Jack said. "Not bad. But still, I move through the trees."

Ned wrote. I WILL BE FINE.

"It is different where we come from," I said. "Being apes, we can travel through trees, if we had trees. Our cities are built so that we can swing from all manner of climbing devices. Of course, we also have cars, ships and planes. Or did. But Suzie Q, you are not going."

"I'm bored," she said.

"No," I said, "you stay here and I'll go."

"Not to worm my way into family situations," Wells said. "But neither you nor Suzie Q should go. Something happens to you, well, she's without her family. And I am stuck with her. No offense."

"I'm offended," Suzie Q said.

Wells shrugged. "Let me say this. I will remain here until the machine is charged, perhaps a little longer. I will measure by the clock here, and I can give you watches to measure time as the sun seems to never move. I have had enough adventure to last a lifetime, and it has given me plenty to write about, and that is what I intend to do. If I go home, I will wait a year from this date, earth time, and I'll return."

"Why not six months?" I said.

"Why not four? Why not two years? I know how it must sound, but I have had enough. I will leave here when the machine is charged. That should be about a week, old earth time. You will have the watches. They keep time and date. If at all possible, I will return a normal earth year from this date, plus a week. At that point, upon return, I will wait another week, in this spot. So, count your days by the watches if you wish to return in a week, and possibly a year. The latter is more up in the air, honestly. I might not want to return, might not be able to. I will make the machine visible if possible. Depending on my situation. But after that, I return home, and I am through forever with traveling through space and time, dimensions and what have you. I merely want a simple life of writing and lecturing. That's my hope."

"You will get it," Jack said.

"You know my future?" Wells asked.

"I know the future of one H. G. Wells," Jack said. "His and yours may be similar."

Wells swallowed. "Tell me no more," he said. "I don't think it's good to know your future."

"Neither do I," Jack said. "But, little friends, if you should manage to keep up with me, which I doubt, I will be putting you into a sticky and possibly unethical situation, stealing the fleece."

"Perhaps they can be reasoned with," I said.

"I doubt they will believe me when I say I merely plan to borrow it, but that would certainly be worth trying. We will see. I mean this politely. I am not a nurse maid. You are companions and I will protect when I can, but I must move swiftly."

"I can also provide you with language translators," Wells said.

I remembered his mention of them.

"Certainly, they work well, as Ned and I both have been injected, and the ability it gives us sometimes causes me to forget that I might not be speaking the same language as someone else, yet I understand them, and they in turn understand me. Ned, of course, can only understand what is spoken. He can't write in any language other than English, so he is only halfway there."

"Indeed, that would be helpful," Jack said. "I have a certain facility with languages, but no doubt that would be a remarkable improvement."

Jack smiled his very good teeth, stuck out his hand, and Wells shook it.

It was my turn. I shook hands with Wells.

"You could stay," he said. "Suzie Q could stay."

"She would be a freak in your world, as you told me. It's best we find our own path."

"Very well," Wells said, leaned down, hugged Suzie Q and kissed her on the top of her head. "You better start packing. I'll get the watches and prepare the injections. And if it was me, I'd bring toilet paper."

Twenty-four

I did just that, packed toilet paper and other items for me and Suzie Q. We got our watches from Wells and took our language shots, started out into a great adventure.

Later, I wished we had stayed in Time Machine. That adventure stuff isn't all it's cracked up to be. Oh. And I plan to tell you just exactly how I became known as Bongo Bill.

Really.

But, we'll come to that in time.

The watches were big turnip watches on chains, and I fastened the chain to my belt and shoved the watch into my goofy pants pocket, because for whatever reason, Suzie Q and I had decided to switch back to our original clown clothing. It just seemed right somehow.

The watch had a gold face that clicked open and inside was a white-faced watch with black hands. Very old-fashioned. Very nice. The language translator business had been painless and quick.

Jack, knowing several languages, tried them all on us, and in my mind, they sounded the same, as if spoken in English.

Very nice.

I should also add that Ned added a horn to his sled. It was a squeeze job. A bulbous balloon that was attached to a brass horn. As we were preparing to start out, he tried it a couple of times. It was loud and awful. It tickled Ned so much he nearly fell off his sled.

It wasn't until we reached the woods and Jack began to trot swiftly ahead of us that it occurred to me that we had no idea where we were going, and that his warning about how hard it would be for us to keep up was solid information.

After the trail in front of us played out and Jack took to the trees, Ned honked the horn on his sled. Me and Suzie Q turned to look.

He held up his slate.

THIS HAS BEEN FUN. I'M GOING BACK TO TIME MACHINE FOR LUNCH. I'M HAVING FISH.

Ned turned his sled and started back.

So much for Ned the bold adventurer.

A Brief Aside and a Look at She Who Must Be Obeyed and Eats Lunch Early

When the time suck happened and Time Machine went one way and Tomi went the other, before that, she was dead at the bottom of the sea, one foot twisted down deep in ancient mud. She spun with the currents, floated with the tall seaweed, because her foot was stuck, turning about in the ooze, but stuck, and then every part of her was soaked in the time suck—let's capitalize that—TIME SUCK, and every part of her was changed, except for her foot, actually her heel, that was the part that was deepest, and it stayed raw and human, but the rest of her did not.

Tomi, soon to be She Who Must Be Obeyed and Eats Lunch Early, came through the gap in time, dislodged finally from the mud, and she jetted down multi-colored, glowing tunnels and arrived Down Under a long time before Time Machine arrived.

It was one of those weird anomalies of time travel. Time Machine went one direction, and Tomi, piggy-backing on the machine's draft, got time-sucked through another gap. She ended up in the same place Wells and his crew were to land a long time later. You might say she had a head start.

The Time Suck pulled the minds of the aliens in the saucer, as well as the living technology of the saucer (that's right, the technology was a living entity), and through a shitty quirk of fate caused by Time Machine itself, all that business went into Tomi.

She breathed big. Her lungs filled. Her brain popped, cells banged together like pool balls. The very fiber of her being altered. She was alive, and she became stuffed tight with weird knowledge, new powers, and a changed appearance made of flesh and bone and alien minds, the technology of the space travelers.

But, alas, just the bad stuff. The primordial part of us and the aliens that is greedy and survivalist and self-destructive. A bit of empathy would have been nice, some logic, but nope, that wasn't on the menu. Not that day. Tomi's buffet of this and that was all the bad stuff.

She could do things. Here's a list.

Knock down anyone who resisted with spurts of blue fulmination from her fingers, spits of fire from her insides. She breathed fire when she so chose, farted jets of blue-white flames. She was strong. She could take a full shot from an arrow and it wouldn't penetrate her skin. She could have taken a full shot from a cannon ball, and it would have bounced. Larger loads of ammunition wouldn't have had much effect either, if any. Of course, there was the one foot that had remained human, but it only itched a little. (Goddamn poison ivy from the World Down Under.)

Yep. She went straight there through the time gap. Unlike Wells and his folk who landed on the surface first, she showed up on the edge of a lake near a beautiful forest ripe with fruits and birds and howling monkeys.

That wouldn't last long, however.

She grew like the proverbial weed in compost and sunlight, jumped up to six feet six. Had shoulders broad as a beer truck. Unknown some-things under her skin crawled and writhed and pushed against her orangish fur as if looking for an exit. There were none at that point in time. The wiggles continued.

She used her powers to decimate the forest around her, killed the monkeys and birds, withered the fruit. She built a strange rolling machine of stone and leather, wood and something odd she regurgitated, all powered by her snapping and popping innards.

Next, she killed people. Wiped out villages and communities. Eventually, she gained followers. Those who realized they couldn't stand against her. The kind of people her father had liked; people who didn't question, or were afraid to.

She made promises. She would rule they world, and they would get the crumbs. Big crumbs. She learned of the fleece, and that became her goal. Her armies grew due to battle wins, brutal murders, destruction, and whip-mean progress.

Machines were built. Smaller than her personal ride. Nice roller wheel about twenty feet across, a throne with a surrey roof and fringe on top, side curtains to roll down when needed, a crapper that her ass fit right into, though it all went down and came out... Where?

On the ground, of course.

The slaves pulled or pushed the machines according to circumstance. Her machine and the other smaller ones, the soldiers, and the ass-whipped, back-scarred slaves, knocked down city walls and rolled over villagers and killed or enslaved them all. They salted fields and shit in wells, burned anything that would catch fire, pushed down trees, climbed up and down mountains, and rolled on.

The slaves were starved thin and covered in mud and dung and parasites. They ate once a day and they didn't always last the day. If one of the slaves fell, didn't get up promptly, then under and into the machine they went. She Who Must Be Obeyed and Eats Lunch Early's personal guard made sure of that, for they were stout and hairy and ripped with muscles like bunched up rocks in too-tight leather bags.

Up a fallen body went, lifted by the powerful hairy arms of her personal guard, tossed into the machines like wheat berries. The grinding stone wheels and cogs turned and turned and crunched and crunched, and the results of those grindings came out at the rear of the machine in shooting shit fashion; gusts of blood and bone and mangled flesh. All of it was gathered in wagons and fed to the slaves, sometimes cooked, sometimes raw, and She Who Must Be Obeyed and Eats Lunch Early, the guard, and the army, always had better food to eat, prepared quite nicely by a mighty fine cook who could make most anything taste like honey and ham. Frequently, he used the same meat the slaves ate, but man, he had spices and could jazz it up and smooth it down. His slave brain soup with a side of bone marrow jelly was divine.

On they rolled, the village of the Golden Fleece in their thoughts and plans; known to be beyond the Blue Mountains in a lush valley full of fine fruits and fields of vegetables, and all manner of goodness.

It had to be destroyed and the fleece had to be taken. The reason for doing that was merely the reason to do it. Sometimes, down deep in her head, like a prehistoric shark, some of Tomi's memories floated up. She remembered when she was young and her father called her ugly and fat, and once when she tried to introduce herself to a boy, and see how that would go, it went bad. She was all dressed up, thought she looked nice, flirty and anxious, but coy, or so she felt.

"I wouldn't fuck you with my next-door neighbor's dog's dick, and that poor fucking dog is dying of some kind of cancer."

It wasn't the sort of response that built self-confidence.

Or her mother saying: "No use looking in the mirror, honey. It's still going to be the same little, fat fuck with a drying cunt thats only use is for peeing."

That hurt.

Tomi tucked it away and let it simmer.

She became bigger and stronger, fatter and meaner, and she began to bully. Rolled her personal shit downhill, let it fall on those she could manage.

And now she was rolling again. But with machinery.

Roll on, roll on.

Villagers fled before them. Monkeys and critters, even the dinosaurs beat feet.

Fear the army and her guard. Fear the rolling dark wood and earth-shined stone machines.

Run, motherfuckers. Run.

And dare not look directly at She Who Must Be Obeyed and Eats Lunch Early, for that is a mortal sin, and to add insult to injury, she was not easy to look at.

She sat high up on the largest machine, having swollen over time. Her head huge and bulbous and her huge naked body fitted tight into straps and board supports and wires and space guy metal from the saucer that had come through with her and had served as her home for a time.

And as the size of the army swelled, so did She Who Must Be Obeyed and Eats Lunch Early. Kept on swelling. She was fed by hoses made of flexible, hollow shafts of vegetation. Sometimes she ate the hoses. She shit through the gap in the machine, splashing the earth beneath her.

Roll on, shit on, roll on, came the songs of the warriors amidst the sound of the lash against the backs and legs of the slaves.

Roll on, shit on, roll on.

—◆—

Let's consider ourselves caught up time wise. She has reached a point where now our heroes, or whatever they are, or turn out to be, are about to cross paths.

Some serious time has passed and She Who Must Be Obeyed and Eats Lunch Early has had time to amass her army and grow nut-ball and turn slime-ball, feed on the bad memories of her life, the anger of the aliens, not to mention the raw power of their machines.

She be funky, baby.

Roll on, shit on, roll on.

Part Two:

*Ned gets hungry, honks his horn and finds a boat,
Tango tells us about himself, there are problems in the
air, Leo is made known and has an adventure of sorts,
and there's a steamboat, and gaseous plants, pits of
sticky oil, and wake up: danger, dinosaurs!*

*There's some other stuff too. Hitch up your drawers
and hang onto your hat. Into the breach we go.*

One

From the Journal of Ned the Seal

The woods were not very comfortable. They were hot and sticky. There were bugs. I decided I didn't want to do it anymore. I had become spoiled by a nice comfortable place void of adventure.

Wells was right. I had seen enough. I wanted Clarence to fix me some hot chocolate. I wanted to live in Time Machine and write stories. I had plenty of stories to tell and could make up the rest of them. I could make up all of them if I wanted to. I didn't want to be eaten by giant birds. The woods were humid and there were bugs. I know. I mentioned that, but it seemed worth repeating. I like air-conditioning.

I was so hungry and in such a hurry to get back to Time Machine, I didn't realize that I had somehow gotten off the main trail. This should not have happened. I had a hard time blaming myself, but finally I had to.

I was lost.

I stopped and considered things.

The sun was no help. It was always in the same place.

I couldn't be that far from Time Machine. I decided to retrace my path. Turning my sled, I started back the way I had come, and then I had a surprise.

It was a large surprise and I could smell it before I could see it. I could hear it too. And when it stepped out of the woods and onto the trail, taking out a couple of large trees as it did, I almost crapped a swirly.

Let me tell you, I have never seen that many teeth, and I have seen a few things in my time as a brain-enhanced seal. It was a multi-colored lizard about twenty-five feet high and six feet wide with a too-large head packed with those teeth I mentioned. It was leaning forward. It had two small, leathery arms that dangled in front of it. It was supported on two fat legs and some large feet with claws at the ends of the toes. It was covered in scales and slime, and as there was a wide spot in the trees above, the sunlight made the slime gleam. I could see there were parasites swimming in the slime. The parasites were almost as big as me.

Did I mention the teeth?

I sat still on my sled and tried to look friendly, though I think I may have looked delicious.

The beast took a deep breath and let it out. That breath, along with the slime on its scaly skin, was the source of the stink.

Its breath could have boiled an egg. It smelled like a giant fart. To make it more uncomfortable, a breeze rustled through the trees and brought the stink right to me.

The dinosaur, or some facsimile of one, took one step, as if it were trying not to break anything precious beneath its foot. And then it took another step with the same carefulness. I realized the dumb beast thought it was sneaking up on me.

I turned my sled, and when it was turned, I began to skootch it forward on the cushion of air and light beneath it, not going too fast, but certainly moving away.

The beast roared. I could hear it tromping after me, no longer bothering with sneaky steps. I gave the sled full throttle. It leaped forward so quickly I was nearly thrown from it. I worked the side mirror switch and the mirrors popped up on either side of the sled. They were full of dinosaur. The beast was licking its lips.

Seals, by the way, are said to be tasty. I thought that was a bit of knowledge you might be interested in knowing, though I provide it as information, not as an ingredient to a recipe.

The path we were on narrowed, which I felt was a good thing for me. I darted between two close-together trees, took a limb in the face that hit me hard enough to make me dizzy, and then I dodged between two other trees that were thankfully wider apart and did not provide a limb to the face.

My plan wasn't as successful as I hoped. The dinosaur hit the trees, one on each shoulder, and they cracked and fell, and they were so tall, they almost hit me. They slammed the ground hard just behind me.

There was a log in front of me and I managed to hit the jump lever and sail over it, just as the monster was about to catch up with me.

The nasty critter caught a foot on the log and tripped and went down, sliding its jaw into the forest mold. I saw this in my mirror and let out a happy bark. I could see that as it got up, ready to go again, there was a change in its appearance that struck me as embarrassment. I patted my butt with my flipper and honked my horn in triumph.

Take that, Doo-doo Breath.

Two

Things were looking good by then, as I had outdistanced my pursuer considerably, but just when I was about to pat myself on the ass again for my own delight, I came to a river. It was a wide river, and on the other side of it there was a great extension of grassland like the one we had landed in when we brought Time Machine through the hole in the world. The grass waved invitingly in the wind.

Now I had a river in front of me and a raging dinosaur behind me. The river wasn't all bad, though, because I can swim like a seal.

That is a seal joke. You might want to write it down. It only works well if you are a seal and you tell it to another seal, or someone who can see you are a seal. So, if you are a seal and you are reading this you might want to write that down, but now that I think about it, I'm the only seal I know of with an enhanced brain that has grafted thumbs and can write. Therefore, the joke might not work with another seal after all.

It is consequently a personal joke.

Ha. Ha.

Anyway, I stopped my sled at the edge of the river and considered. I could ease across the water to safety without having to swim like a seal. My sled would carry me across. But, I was suddenly overwhelmed with a realization. I was deeply lost. I had no idea where I was, how I had come to the river, or where Time Machine was. Was the grass across the river related to the field of grass where Time Machine was?

Still, a river led somewhere, and I didn't really have a choice. I was about to cross on my sled, when I heard the beast roar and crash through the trees and underbrush behind me. I wasn't quite as far ahead of the monster as I had assumed.

I checked the mirrors.

Yep. One big dinosaur. And it was close. I had spent too much time pondering on the bank of the river trying to make some kind of decision.

I gunned the machine forward, began to glide over the water. The dinosaur hit the water behind me, and was making good splashing time, as the river was not deep there.

If I had been any more frightened I would have offered myself to the beast. It beat being terrified.

Or so I thought for about ten seconds, but after further evaluation, decided that being eaten was worse than being terrified. It was higher on the bad scale.

I could still hear the big creature splashing in the water behind me, and now I could feel its hot breath on my back. I had the sled cranked way up, but the dinosaur was gaining.

I looked in my mirrors and confirmed this. I was about to be a nice appetizer for the monster. That's when there was a loud splash, and the dinosaur dropped out of sight.

I turned for a look.

It had found a deep part of the river and had gone under. It was struggling fiercely to regain footing that wasn't there.

I sailed on to the other side. I spun the sled and looked back at the river. I was delighting in the beast drowning.

Does that make me a bad seal?

Then I realized it was not going to drown.

A very large creature with a long neck and massive flippers, with about as many teeth as the dinosaur that had been chasing me, surfaced and snapped its long neck out like a whip and grabbed the struggling creature by the head.

The monsters roared together, and then the one that had been chasing me disappeared beneath the water with a titanic splash, its hind feet being the last thing seen. The water rippled, and then it rippled less, and finally it was still. The water turned red, and the red spread.

Well, that was it. Both of those creatures were down under, and one of them was lunch and the other was a diner.

After a moment of relief, I was still hungry and I was still lost, not to mention confused. I couldn't imagine how I had gotten so far off the trail. It had seemed like a straight shot back to me.

But at least I hadn't been eaten.

Score one for the seal team.

Three

I sledded along the side of the river. It was loud there, because the birds were excited. I thought it was due to the dinosaurs. All the noise they had made in the river. And then I realized it was not entirely about the dinosaurs. It had to do with a cookout.

There was a half dozen wild-haired looking people on the beach. They were burned red by the sun, and there was a fire and they were gathered around it, and the guest of honor was burned black by the blaze, except for the teeth which shone white and shiny. They were turning him on a spit supported by two large pieces of wood that had been buried in the ground and were forked at the top. The spit fit in that.

I could see that lunch was human-shaped but had a tail. Then I realized all those people had tails, the tips of which had tufts of bright red hair. My mind had not wrapped around it at first, as I thought it was part of their clothing, but they weren't wearing clothing. The meal on the spit was well cooked. I could see a sprig or two of hair on its head and its balls were withered by the fire. A woman was reaching over to cut off his blackened balls and weiner with a rugged-looking knife.

She tasted the meat carefully and made a happy moan, and then the others set to the meal, cutting pieces with their knives. They were so involved with their feast, they hadn't noticed me.

I turned my sled and started back up the beach.

That's when I heard someone yell.

Shit. They had seen me. I glanced back hoping they would stick to their meal, but no, that wasn't their way. They were coming after me, running fast, their tails lifted and waving behind them like flags. The woman who had cut off the balls was in the lead, breasts flapping. She was a fast runner. She had the meat in her mouth and the penis flopped.

I passed where I had come out of the water and cruised on beyond that. The sled was swift and I was making good time, but the people behind me weren't quitters. I presumed that the idea of adding a seal to their picnic was foremost on their minds.

That's when I saw a boat. It wasn't a big boat and it had oars and there was a mast and a collapsed sail as well. I could have used my sled to cross the river, but I could see that the boat was supplied with baskets and barrels, and I thought some of them might contain food, though my appetite wasn't as sharp at that moment as it was before I saw the revolting meal those cannibals were having.

I took a chance and floated my sled onto the boat and settled it. They were still coming, but I had the lead on them. I pushed off with a pole that was in the boat, which considering I have flippers with thumbs, was not all that easy. Once I got the boat pushed away from the shore, I sat in the center and took hold of both oars and started trying to oar my way out to the center of the river. Again, I have flippers, so it was a bit awkward, but I was getting the job done.

I wasn't far out when they reached the spot where the boat had been and they began wading into the river. I continued to work the oars as best I could.

They were swimming for me now, and for a moment I thought I might have to use my sled again and abandon the boat, ride across the river on that.

But, I realized several things in a row.

This was the boat they had come in, and they had left it unprotected to make a fire at a clearer spot up the river. So, I had that going for me.

Second, I had just enough of a lead to stay ahead of them, and finally, the river had grown deep and all they could do now was swim after me, and I was moving much more briskly than they were.

Eat rat poo, I thought.

I kept rowing. The current had caught me by then, and it was moving me rapidly along. I had no idea where I was going, but I let it pull me. I hauled the oars inside and set about raising the sail, calculating the wind.

The sail fluttered and blustered and away I went, pulling the sail cords, setting it just right for the moment, switching it when the wind changed. I had learned about sailing, at least a little, on previous adventures.

I turned my ass to those on the bank and bumped it in the air a couple of times. Bet they wanted a piece of that. Well cooked, of course.

I don't want to sound like a complainer, but that wind was cold. I am no longer used to cold. Or heat. Or hunger. I am spoiled, no doubt.

I wondered about the people on the banks of the river. Who were they? Why were they eating someone? Did they know their lunch? Had he died and been put on the menu, or had he been killed? Did they cook him with potatoes? I hadn't seen any. Would there be dessert?

Didn't really matter, but I'm a curious kind of seal.

Four

Beyond the shore on either side was mostly jungle. Steam due to humidity rose from it and coasted out over the water.

The sun didn't move, but I noticed it was growing darker. The darkness came with a wind and the darkness was an oily flow of clouds. Gradually the clouds became thicker and they were low down, sailing over the water, and I could feel their damp weight, like someone had dipped cold cotton in ink. The air grew even colder. I hadn't expected darkness at all, not with an eternal sun, but the clouds were providing just that. I knew I had to get off the river, because to continue down it in the dark could be as dangerous as what might be on shore or in the jungle. Out here were unknown currents, unseen rocks, and of course there were aquatic dinosaurs. I had seen one drag a dinosaur of good size down under.

Although it was growing dark due to the clouds, I could still see a little, and one of the things I saw was a dark strip of land off to my right.

The wind was still strong, so I worked the sails and sailed in that direction. The sails blustered and my little boat began to move rapidly through the water.

When I was close to shore, I collapsed the sails and took to the oars. I hate the oars. But, as before, I did it, and soon I was on shore. The boat was too heavy to pull up on land, but I leaped in the water and swam behind it and used my head to push it, and eventually it was on the shoreline.

I clambered back into the boat and floated out over it on my sled. I started to cruise along the river bank. I hadn't gone far when it grew even darker; those blowing black clouds now thick as a wool coat. I used the light on the sled to make my way back to the boat, settled the sled down inside of it, and finally, even though I was hungry still, I laid down and hoped something wouldn't find me and eat me.

I could smell a sour smell coming from the baskets in the boat, but I didn't let it trouble me. I was exhausted. I grew marginally comfortable and slept. I dreamed of fish.

Nothing ate me.

At some point the black clouds had blown out, and after the exhaustion passed, I lay cold and shivering in the bottom of the damp boat until being uncomfortable brought me awake. I missed my bunk in Time Machine. I missed Wells. I missed Clarence and his hot chocolate. I missed my books and my chess set.

It was once again a bright yellow day, and as there was no wind, I began to warm up. Normally, I would have enjoyed going into the water, but I was not anxious to swim in a river packed with monsters, even though I wanted a fish.

I looked in the baskets in the boat, hoping for food.

There was an arm. A highly unattractive head. A small basket of testicles and weiners, and I mean the kind that go with the testicles. None of this struck me as appetizing, and after seeing what was in the baskets, I set them over the side, watched them float a distance, become saturated with water, and sink.

There was a leather bag of water, and I drank from that. I might as well have sipped directly from the river, which is possibly where the bagged water came from. It tasted dirty and sour. I only allowed myself one or two sips and hoped it wouldn't cause me to shit all over everything in the boat.

I looked through the other baskets, but it was more cannibal stuff, except for some fish heads. I ate those. Wells says it's disgusting to eat the heads, but I like fish, though I prefer them not to have been dead for days. But a somewhat aged fish eyeball is quite the delicacy. I really like fish.

I don't know if I've mentioned that.

I decided now I could use the sled to explore. The boat had been a big help, because the sled must rest a bit now and then to stay at its prime. The batteries recharge themselves. It is a very nice invention. It was kind of the way Time Machine worked, but the sled recharged much faster. At its lowest, it was always able to move a little. If I went at a low speed, it hardly used energy at all, but going fast and crossing rivers caused it to bleed off power more quickly. It took more energy for it to stay afloat over water. The sun was its master, but there was plenty of sunlight here, even though there had been the temporary clouds.

I climbed on the sled and flicked the switch that brought it to life, worked the little toggle that guided it. It lifted easily out of the boat and I began to glide along the bank. I thought if I could find a gap in the forest where there was sunlight, I could give my sled a deep charge and then I was ready for anything.

Almost anything.

I cruised along, watching.

I very badly wanted to honk the horn, but that seemed a ridiculous and possibly dangerous idea, so I did not.

Well, maybe once.

One

From the Diary of Jack Bloomingdale, Tango, Duke of the Jungle, Man with a Tan

In short time, when I looked back, my companions were no longer visible. The forest had swallowed them up. For now, they would be okay, and they could easily return to the clearing and the time craft, but it was necessary that I move on, and move fast.

Their fate was their choice. Or as we used to say when I was growing up with the ape men, as others refer to them, "It's your limb to fall off of."

When the trail through the forest became thin, I took to the trees, swung from limb to limb, vine to vine, covering space faster than I might have had I tried to stay on the ground and work my way through the trees, brush and thorns, and what have you. High up was a highway of greenery and up there is one hell of a view.

I passed chattering monkeys, exactly like those that had once been on the top world, as well as other types I had never seen before. I didn't know this world totally, not yet, but what I knew of it was amazing. Everything we had managed to hunt to extinction, kill through waste of environment and greed, was here. It was a beautiful world, green and moist, and food was plentiful. The population of humans and near-humans was substantial, but nothing like what you might have found above when humans covered the earth, before things went bad in many ways and they died in droves. So far, the humans here took only what they needed, and were too primitive to know that they were missing out on fast cars, coal, oil, gas, video games and pork belly futures. They killed each other a lot, though. A self-destruct human trait.

Perhaps those here could profit by more knowledge, but from my experience above, knowledge hadn't helped much. The obvious was ignored, and greed was deeply and happily embraced. But greed, like a big snake, like blind acceptance of religion or leaders of any kind, can turn on you. Just give it time.

I moved rapidly until it was nearly sunset, and then I looked back and saw that Bill and his sister Suzie Q were coming through the trees in my fashion. They were apes, I should have realized they would have an advantage to humans. Still, I was somewhat surprised at how quickly they came. Perhaps that was due to a bit of conceit on my part.

I broke out some food from my pack, perched on a limb, ate, and waited for them to show up. They eventually arrived. Their fur was covered in little broken limbs and leaves and they looked exhausted. They didn't bother to eat, but they did drink from their canteens.

"You have done well," I said, as they found a spot on one of the limbs, leaned against the tree trunk to rest. "What of Ned?"

"He got hungry for fish and went back to the machine."

I laughed at that. "And you?"

"We have decided to continue. At home, we travel through the cities on metal limbs and vines, but this is far harder. The pack is heavy and catches on things, and it's hot," Bill said.

"It won't always be," I said. "Frequently arctic winds blow in from the roof of the world and rustle through the trees. It will be cold then and the leaves will rattle like maracas. It may even be dark as night."

"Night?" Bill said.

"Of a sort. Clouds go black and blow in and drop down close to the ground. They are sometimes very thick, and at other times less so. There is no specific time they appear. I'm not sure what causes it. They don't always come, but I have been here long enough I can feel them before they show up. You get a sense for the weather, a barometer in your bones. The chill wind is coming soon and the dark will come with it. As for the cold, as you go farther away from the arctic hole, deep into the jungle, it warms up considerably. Everything becomes harder. Dangerous animals, snakes, bugs big enough to straddle a wild hog flat-footed, and of course tribes and creatures that want to kill you, which, as you might recall, is how I ended up on that mud mound."

"What did you do to make them mad?" Suzie Q said.

"I know you are looking for a more complex and satisfying answer, but it is still the same. I crossed their land. I made the mistake of allowing myself to rest too deeply, for I was exhausted from having combat with humans and shortly thereafter, a sabre tooth. I managed to kill many humans and then elude them, and shortly thereafter I knocked the sabre tooth unconscious after a heated battle, but I was weakened. I knew from observing from a tree that there was a settlement nearby, and I might have chosen to go around it, but I did not.

"Tribes here are protective of their locale. Not too unlike how it was above. It was a mistake I knew better than to make, but make it I did, and grab me they did. They sacrifice a lot. It's how they think they bring good things to them. It does not, however, bring good things to the captives. The others, they had been there the day before. I was new meat. Thanks to you and your companions, I still live. Rest now. Within a short time, I'm moving on. You may come or not, but I suggest not, and I tell you true as the ground has dirt, I cannot wait on you."

"We understand," Bill said.

"Do we?" Suzie Q said.

"We must," Bill said.

"Yes," I said. "You must."

Two

They groomed themselves for a while, eating the insects they found in their fur, and then they rested. I hadn't expected that. I felt they were probably too sophisticated for that, but I guessed wrong. I think it was comfort food and a comfort mannerism. They would find many things disgusting, but the one thing many would find disgusting, they did not; eating live insects.

I left them sound asleep in the tree. I swung from limb to limb, from vine to vine, and soon the forest was a deep flood of shadowed green beneath me. The black clouds rolled in and covered the sun and left the world in darkness.

At that point I had to stop. I couldn't see my hand in front of my face. It had turned cool as well. I removed the bathrobe from my pack and hung my pack on a limb. I stood up on the limb where I intended to sleep and put on the bathrobe. It was thick and comfortable and warm. I sat down with my back against the tree trunk and pulled my knees up so that the robe would fall over my bare legs.

I wondered about the two furry ones for a moment, and then I slept. I dreamed gently of my woman and of the fleece and of the world above, gone more savage than here; a world that had turned insane. I was glad I left it. Rather to be eaten by lions than to be nibbled to death by mice.

Three

I had arrived in this dangerous world some time ago with Jill, though exactly how long ago I was uncertain. Time was odd in Down World. By surface time I might have been here thirty years, or three hundred, though admittedly that was unlikely.

Time is of no consequence to one like me and my mate Jill. We were long-lived, perhaps immortal. Old age was our bitch. Of course, injury or disease could still take us out. That was the problem. For a goodly stretch, and my inner clock estimated a month Up World or Above World time, I had been pursuing the fleece. That was a long time for someone to be sick, and my only consolation was that the disease was not painful, was slow acting, and people seldom died quickly of it, and someone of Jill's nature would most likely last much longer than the average human.

When she got sick, after all other means were tried, I set out in search of the fleece. Before that there had been much adventure and discovery, now everything I saw seemed muted and dull, no matter what the situation. With Jill sick, a part of me was sick too. Being long-lived, we were not monogamist. We had taken lovers, both of us. This was merely to satisfy sexual desire. Still, we were dedicated to one another and saw our mating for life, however long it must be. I knew that the thought of her dying was the most painful thought of my already long life; she made me whole. I know that sounds like romantic clap-trap, but there you have it. My honest feelings about Jill.

There were moments when I wished we had not come to Down World, but those were moments when I was thinking about the sickness. As far as I knew, the disease only existed here. But to have stayed in Up World would have drained our souls. If we were to die, it was better in this hidden world than above. At least here when people wanted to kill you it was straightforward, not dressed up in politics or religion, administered with fists and weapons, not the stroke of a pen or the tap of a key.

Here's how it started for me, my adventures Down Under.

We had come down from the earth above by zeppelin, me and Jill, and we had many adventures here, and then, and then, somehow, she got the sickness. For whatever reason, I did not.

I was in the act of freeing a village of folks terrorized by a giant ape when she got sick. I didn't know this at the time, as I was about my mission. I managed to tranquilize the ape, and on a giant raft, with help from the villagers, I transported him by river to a deep valley where there was all manner of huge beasts and lots of trees and water and lots of food for a giant ape to eat. The walls of the valley were slick and impossible to climb. I closed the path to the river that tumbled over a great waterfall, so the ape and the other creatures, far larger than the dinosaurs we frequently encountered, could not escape. The water still tumbled over the falls, but the areas around it, the former paths out of the great valley, were eliminated. The creatures there, and my suspicion was there were no humans, had their own world in that great gorge. A place where humans couldn't bother them. A place where the jungle grew thick and food of all sorts was available.

It was my thought that sometime in the future, Jill and I would move there and make it our home. Down World was better than Up World, but in time I suspected humans would do as humans do, and we would grow weary of them, and only want to be to ourselves in that hidden valley.

That was my thought when I finished closing the exits from the valley, but when I arrived back at the village, I was informed that Jill was sick. It was a disease that hit the village from time to time, but only one or two would get it, but this time there was only one, and it was my beloved, Jill. I presumed that the inhabitants of the village had mostly built up a resistance, because it was usually only the young and the old that died of the disease. Healthy adults of middling age rarely got it.

Jill was an outsider, however, and as strong as she was, as resistant as she was to most things, she had gone weak-kneed, and then had fallen into a deep sleep. As I said. I admit I thought she might have been poisoned purposely with the disease. The person I suspected of it disappeared from the village, perhaps realizing I would be suspicious of him. He had tried to woo her and failed. Even though Jill and I are what you might say unconcerned with conventional sexual morality, we are dedicated to one another, and we do not pursue such liaisons when we are living together, but only when we have long separations, and considering our life span, we have at times been apart for as long as a year or more.

The long and the short of it was, she didn't fancy him and he was rebuked, and I made it clear to him that his one attempt was the end of it, and, of course, Jill being able to take care of herself, told him the same. You should see that woman fight or swing naked through the trees. It is a sight.

Later this rejected man's bones were found near the village. He had encountered a sabre tooth. Fair enough. It was highly possible he had somehow passed a diseased body part from one of the villagers to her through her food, ground up a piece of contaminated lung or liver and managed to pollute something she ate. On the other hand, his disappearance and death by tiger could have been a coincidence. No matter. I didn't like him. I'm glad he's dead.

Poor, beautiful Jill.

I remember looking at her lying in the great bed in the house I had built with my own hands, the one where the roof could swing open, and the sides of the house could fold down into a compact pile, giving us sunlight and wind when we wanted it. I would sit by her bed with its white sheets, the white covers pulled up to her chin, her blond hair cascading around her head like gold fire, her face expressionless, but beautiful, her lips slightly parted, showing her white teeth, and I would put my head to her chest, listen, hear her heart beat, feel mine sink, and when no one was looking, the Duke of the Jungle cried.

It was not long after, as I fretted by her bedside, not sleeping, not eating, that I learned of the fleece from elders in the village. I knew about the aliens, of course. I knew too from other travels to alternate universes and different time lines, that at the same time aliens invaded here, they were invading other worlds, universes and dimensions.

The aliens were not always the same. They were alternate too, but the invasions ran simultaneously. There are a lot of time quirks, and one of them is that frequently, but not always, an event happening on one earth is akin to an event happening on an alternate earth. Sometimes the same people show up in other time lines, though not always.

There was a legend about this alien fleece, golden and thick, and it was enticing. Certainly, I thought it might be nothing more than myth, but since the fleece and the creature it once covered came from somewhere out beyond the stars, who was to say? The alien itself was said to have been an amazing being, so might not its fleece have powers as the legend suggested?

It was something I had to consider. It was all that was left to consider, and on the day Jill's breathing slowed and her breath turned sweet, like the beginnings of jungle rot, and after all available medicines had been tried, those I had brought with me from the world above, and those the healers had available in Down World, I knew, for the first time in my life, real fear.

We had come to this world from the world up there by zeppelin, and it was now my desire to go up in it again, to sail over this world and speed my path toward the fleece.

I did just that. I had my captain, Leo Carter, a young black man, short and strong, built like a boxer. He had actually been a boxer. Middleweight. His face was smooth because he rarely took a hard shot. He could move quickly and he could hit quickly, and he could hit hard. He was smart and could work any kind of machinery and build things out of little to nothing. Once with a pocket knife he whittled a wooden screwdriver and we used it to escape a very nasty situation, but that is another story.

The important thing was he lived there in the village with us, having happily abandoned the Above World, and he was always willing to be my partner in adventure.

With weapons and supplies, we set out. Among our weapons were a few guns, but mostly I had what I was most comfortable with. A supply of bows and quivers full of arrows, long spears tipped with steel brought from above.

The wind was gentle, and the zeppelin held its helium well and it rode smooth. We pointed it in the direction of the Blue Mountains. It was said the village of the Rumwara was on its far side, and there, in their village, I would find the fleece, either to borrow or to steal.

Of one thing I was certain. I would bring it back.

Four

Me and Leo sailed the skies. We sailed beneath that permanent sun, the wind smooth for days as we piloted farther away from the arctic mouth, and I should add that there are several gaps in Up World that lead to Down World. Some are obvious, some less so. The village where Jill and I stayed was near a gap where the ocean washed down and came to rest below in a vast dark sea near a sandy shore with a thick jungle just beyond, and deep within it, the village where we lived.

But there is always wind down below, winds from above, cold or warm or hardly felt, and it was on that wind that we started out. The inky clouds came from time to time, but still we sailed by compass and instinct inside their darkness. When the clouds passed, we kept our course by sight and instruments, by heart and soul.

And then things turned bad.

Bright and sunny a day as you could wish for, as all of them are until the clouds and the storms fueled from above come, blustering across our hidden world, wet and windy.

We were reasonably close to mountains, if judged by flying distance and speed. We could see them clearly as we coasted over a vast expanse of water, an inland sea. The sea was shiny as polished silver. And then, there was a nudge against the craft, like a hand had pushed us. It was not like the dark clouds of before or the brisk winds that gave us speed. It was a great whirling wind and a black as death cloud. We were lifted, and we began to spin, around and around in a sack of darkness.

I rushed to the control room to find Leo fighting the controls, and he was losing the battle. Around and around the zeppelin went, flinging me against the walls, one side, then the other. I crawled to one of the chairs in front of the fore window.

There were odd cracks of light in the dark cloud, and when those cracks were there, I could see fish and even a small aquatic dinosaur trying to swim in the whirling water and air. In an instant, I knew we were caught up in a massive water spout. A wind from the arctic shafts had met a warmer wind and mixed with the water and it had made the air and water swirl. The water rose up just as we passed above; rose up and nabbed us. We were in the center of the swirl.

"Hang on, Jack," Leo yelled, as if this was advice I might need.

The swirl continued, and we drifted away from the center toward one of the twirling walls, and then there was a popping sound, like someone had stuck a needle in a balloon—a massive balloon—and then there was a spewing, sputtering sound like a creeping fart, and then we no longer had power. We no longer had a zeppelin. What we had was like a giant prophylactic that nature had used up and was discarding into the sea.

It happened quick, once the whirl discarded us. We hit the water, and the zeppelin bag, and all the innards of the craft, collapsed around us. I was not so much frightened, as disappointed. We would not be able to find the fleece and bring it to Jill. I had not only lost mine and Leo's life on this quest, I had effectively ended Jill's as well.

The impact was vicious, but the rubber skin that made up the great balloon bag cushioned our crash to some degree, as we had turned upside down and it landed first.

Water was running in at all points, and down into the wet we went. I sucked in a deep breath. I could see the glass before the control board in a last flash of instrument light. The glass wobbled but held. I saw Leo float by. He looked at me. His face was not filled with fear. There was a wry look to his dark features, like a man that had just discovered what he had eaten was not, as assumed, a pickle.

That last little light in the wheelhouse died out.

At that moment, holding my breath, I was on the verge of having to accept death. It would have been easy to do, but I am not built that way.

I could no longer see Leo, but I swam in the direction I assumed him to be after my last sighting, and it was an accurate choice. I felt out and touched him, and then I grabbed him. The deflated zeppelin churned and turned in the water. We were upside down now, but I could still see the view glass as the dark had passed and sunlight was reaching down through the water. The only real space left in the zeppelin was the control room, framed as it was with wood and light metal. I swam hard for the view glass, kicked at it where I had seen it try to buckle.

That would be the weak point.

It didn't come loose.

I kicked it repeatedly, harder with each kick. I felt my energy flag. I kicked one more time. The glass came undone and then the water caught it, peeled it open. I swam behind it, pulling Leo after me.

The water was clear, and I could see the craft below us, lit by the powerful penetrating sunlight. It had wadded up into a giant ball, was drifting down like a dying, wrinkled whale. Wreckage floated out of the window and out of other gaps, and then the craft spun down into deeper water where the light didn't shine, and I could no longer see it.

I looked up, swam toward the light. Leo was mostly limp in my grasp, but now and again he kicked with his feet, trying to help me rise us out of the depths.

The light grew brighter, then brighter still, and just as I thought my lungs would burst, we surfaced. The sunlight was warm for a moment, and then the colder waters of the sea took over. I shivered.

Leo wasn't breathing. I slapped his chest a few times, that being the best I could do under the circumstances, but it had the proper effect. He spat water, began to breathe again.

After a moment, he came alert. I let him go and we swam side by side in the direction of the shore. But that wasn't a swim we were going to make easy.

At the time, we both wore clothes. I was not wearing my loin cloth underneath, as I occasionally did when entering the jungle of the upper world, or this one down under. I took off my shirt, rebuttoned it, tied it securely at the bottom, whipped it over my head and collected air in it. Leo copied me.

It's an old Navy survival trick. It made a momentary float device, a kind of cheap-ass life preserver. It gave us a breather, but we had to repeat the process a number of times as the air would seep out no matter how hard you tried to hold it in. After a bit, the material was just too soaked to gather air anymore.

I hung the shirt over the back of my neck and shoulders, thinking it might come in handy later, and we began to swim again.

"I don't think we'll make it, Jack," Leo said.

"You are never finished until you are," I said.

"I may be finished," he said. "I can't feel my legs. The water has made them numb."

I pulled my shirt off my neck and shoulders and had him take hold of one end of it. I swam with one hand and kicked my feet, pulled him along. I think it should go without mentioning that I am incredibly strong. No exaggeration, just an evaluation.

Still, as time wore on, without the movement of the sun, I began to think perhaps merely believing that you are not finished isn't the same as not being finished.

I was considering the grim reality of our prospects when the beast floated up.

It was a sea beast, whale-like, but with a long neck that dangled under water, and when I ducked my head under for a look, I saw a narrow head full of teeth was attached to that neck. It was narrow but it was still quite large. The good news was the creature was dead and bloated. It had somehow been loosened from its tomb below, perhaps by our damaged zeppelin.

Suddenly, we had a methane-packed death bag that we could ride one. Fate was with us in that moment. I felt like it owed us on, but the flat and obvious truth is the cosmos isn't aware of you and doesn't give a shit if you live or die or make the baseball team.

Leo and I scrambled on top of the beast, which was in fact its belly, for it was turned on its back. We could feel the methane inside shift, and we could feel guts shift, and finally we found our places and sat still, letting the sun warm our bodies.

We were exhausted and decided to lie down and rest. Before lying down, we took off our pants and underwear, Leo removed his shirt. The socks and shoes had come off naturally with all the swimming. I still had my shirt in my hand. We laid them out to dry. Beside them, we stretched out on the great body and let the sun warm us.

We lay there for a long time.

Five

I awoke to the stink of the decaying creature, and the sound of birds squawking in the distance. Leo was beginning to stir. Our clothes had dried, but they smelled bad. The odor from the body of the beast had soaked into them.

I stood up and begrudgingly put on my clothes. I didn't really want to wear them, but I felt I might need the cloth for something.

Looking out over the water, I could see a line of land in the distance. It was several miles away, and the body of the beast appeared to be floating in that direction. Perhaps it would float near enough we could swim to shore, or it might even beach itself, so we could ride it in like a boat.

"I feel better," Leo said, sitting up, "but I'm hungry."

"We could eat some of this beast, but I don't have a knife, and even if we did tear into it, it would be letting the air out of our life raft, similar to what happened with the zeppelin."

Leo made a face that nearly twisted his dark skin into a knot. He shook his head.

"I'm not eating this thing. It's rotting."

"Then you are not truly hungry," I said.

"If I was, eating it would surely make me sick."

"It depends on how rotten the internal organs are. I've eaten food many times that some would call spoiled. I grew up with apes who ate anything they could find. Mostly vegetarian, but they'd eat meat when it was available, and they could be scavengers."

"You're right, Jack. I'm not that hungry yet."

I smiled at him. "Neither am I, but still, I could eat."

"I'd like to eat, but I'd prefer something fresh. I can even do raw in some cases, but rotten? I'd prefer not to."

We sailed for a long time, and eventually I did truly become thirsty and hungry. The water in this inland sea was not salty, so we could drink that, but I wasn't sure how Leo would react. There could be germs in the water that he didn't have a resistance to. I, on the other hand, was not prone to easy sickness. I had a lot of built-in protections, both genetic and environmental, and much of it due to the longevity potion. I could acquire a disease, as I've said, but I wasn't prone to it. I had lived a great many years, and had rarely been sick, and never in a dangerous way. I could even function well when sick. No exaggeration, just a revelation of facts.

Then again, Jill was the same, and she had fallen ill. It was one reason I suspicioned poison.

Eventually we saw above us a gathering of birds. The ones that would later plan to feast on me while I was tied to that mound of mud. But, all this, of course, is before that, but in this moment in time, they were no less aggressive.

There was a flock of them, and they had been attracted to the monster corpse. From time to time they flew close, checking out their possible meal.

"Be still, Leo," I said. "Do not move."

Eating a fresh dead bird would be a lot better than eating the rotting monster, so I began to make plans to capture one.

We sat still and the birds came closer, and finally one came very close. It was huge. It could have tucked a bald eagle under one of its wings. Its shadow was as large as light aircraft.

I breathed shallowly, and Leo tried to follow my example. He did well, but I could hear his breathing as clearly as listening to a bass drum being beat.

I assumed the birds could hear him as well. But their hunger was causing them to chance it, and they were big birds and not frightened easily. They were birds of prey.

And then one of them came close enough that I leaped up and grabbed its leg with both hands and tried to pull it down so that I might kill it by breaking its neck.

It proved stronger than I anticipated.

I struggled with it as it beat its wings and began to lift me off the corpse. Leo jumped up and grabbed my waist and pulled. The both of us pulled, but the bird kept beating its wings and it began to gain altitude with me clutching its leg, and Leo with his arms around my waist.

We were lifted and carried away from the corpse. For a moment, I felt a sense of disappointment. I had become attached to our raft and missed it as you might a nice hotel room you had been in for a few days. Even as a man of the jungle, there were times when there was nothing I appreciated more than a good hotel bed and room service.

Other birds swooped in, trying to peck us with their beaks. With Leo hanging to my waist, I lifted my feet and kicked out at them, even hit one hard enough in the head I heard bones snap. It fell from the sky, going around and around like a top, and then it hit the water in an explosion of colorful feathers that shot out from its body like arrows.

Up and up we went, the birds flashing all about us, and then I saw we were heading toward land. The bird was growing weak. It was struggling now. Its wings beat less often, and it was flying lower, gliding a lot. My six-foot-five frame, my two hundred and thirty-five pounds of bone and muscle, blood and internal organs, plus Leo's solid weight of probably one hundred and ninety pounds, had finally worn it down.

It flew low. It was almost to the shore, but the shore might still be too high for us to drop once we reached it, and we would after that quickly be over a vast jungle, and to fall into it would certainly be deadly. The result being us broken up amongst the branches, perhaps pierced by limbs, or if we were lucky we would fall into some gap between the trees and be killed quick and clean by impact with the ground.

"Let go, Leo," I said. "Let go. We are going into the water again. We must."

Leo hesitated slightly, then let go. It was a long fall, but not so bad that we would be shattered. Not if we kept our legs straight and entered the water like an arrow.

I saw Leo drop and hit the water in this fashion, and then I let go a moment later, so as not to land on him.

Down I went, into the water and under. The water was cold. I had momentarily forgotten that. When I surfaced, I looked up and our bird was gone. I turned and could see Leo, and way out in the water, the birds were thick on our corpse raft, feasting.

It was a short swim to shore, and we both made it. We lay on the sand for a long time and warmed in the central sun. Leo slept, but I did not. I felt we might be in greater danger on land than in the water, or certainly the danger would at least be equal in proportion.

Six

I took the time while Leo slept to make a crude spear that I sharpened by breaking it so that it made a point. It was not a strong point, but it was something.

I made another for Leo. The clothes I wore stank so much, I stripped them off and washed them at the shoreline, squeezing out the stink. I hung them on low-hanging limbs near the shore and let the eternal sunlight dry them.

When Leo awoke, he did as I had done, and washed his clothes and hung them to dry. When mine were dry, I turned my shirt into a loin cloth, and decided to tear the pants into strips. I tied the strips around my waist, as did Leo. Strips of cloth can come in handy.

We then sought out food by wading into the water and using our spears to stick fish. We had no way to conveniently make a fire, so I tore the fish open and we ate the speared flesh raw. It was a sweet enough fish, so we managed it without problem, though I was curious how Leo would deal with it. I must say he did quite well.

When we felt full and rested, we started down a jungle trail. I had lost sight of the mountains that had been my guide, and I found a tall tree in the jungle, climbed it, and stood at its summit and looked out. I could see the tips of the blue-ridged mountains from there, and once I could do that, I could easily chart a course in my head. Once I had the destination in mind, I memorized certain aspects of the jungle that I knew would become my guide. I could also see what appeared to be a massive ant hill in the distance, and I felt that would be our first marker; it was impossibly large for an ant hill, but I had learned a lot of things in this world were impossibly large, why not ants and their domain? I could see slight movement, but not recognize its source.

There were tendrils of mist or smoke rising up from the mound. That too was not entirely clear, nor could I explain it.

It was then that fate took an unexpected hand.

As we entered the jungle one of those storms that happened from time to time, and had been the cause of our current situation, came about, and this one brought cold rain and churned it through the jungle trees and carried with it dark clouds; the dark clouds twisted and rolled and were low to the earth.

"Not again," Leo said.

"Again," I said, thinking that as we moved farther from the polar gaps, perhaps the weather would be stabilized. So far, this was not the case.

It was a terrible rain, and we climbed a tall tree with thick limbs and sat on a big limb with our backs against the tree trunk. It was not dry, but the leaves were thick and the limbs around and above us were thick as well, so it served some purpose, though the wind nearly knocked us off our perch as it rattled the leaves and vibrated the limbs. Birds nested near us, and down below we could hear a stampede of animals. It seemed for a time we might weather the storm, when suddenly there was a cracking sound and the clouds around us were so dark it was as if we had been sacked.

The cracking sound was our tree, which had seemed so sturdy. It pitched and twisted and flung us out of it.

In the dark I couldn't see Leo. I couldn't see myself. I was flung hard against trees and floating debris, and I fought to maintain the surface of what I realized was a flood. I could feel creatures, both aquatic and terrestrial, swimming all around me.

Eventually the clouds cracked and the locked sun shone through. I was in fast-moving water, and there were animals and aquatic creatures beside me. Big ones, but they weren't paying me any mind. They were struggling the same as I was, swimming for their life.

But that's when I realized I had lost Leo, and, of course, I feared the worst.

After a brief time, it was like someone had pulled the plug on a drain, for the flood flowed faster, and the water went lower. I grabbed a tree limb and clung to it momentarily before climbing up higher above the rushing waters.

From up there I looked for Leo, but he was not in sight. I waited there until the water lowered even more and then turned to wet tendrils. The little water trails rustled along the heavily mulched earth, and finally wound out of sight and the land cleared.

I climbed down, and looked for Leo for a long time, but had to resolve the worst had happened. I had no choice but to move on. I was heavy of heart, but soon put the feelings aside. Having grown up in the jungle and having been raised by apes, I had seen a lot of violence, sudden death, and it was part of the experience that you grieved and moved on. It's what you did. You were a living organism and your job was to keep living when you had done all you could do. I wasn't without feelings, but to survive I couldn't let them rule me. It was my nature to move on and survive. Jill, of course, might have been a different case. She was my Achilles' heel, and I hers.

I did move on, leaving the damage of the flood behind me, walking with my feet and ankles burying up in the mud. There were dead animals all around me and flopping fish. I stopped to break open one of the fish and eat it. It gave me renewed strength. I found a fallen tree with strange yellow fruit on its limbs. Birds were pecking at some of the fruit, which led me to believe that it was not poisonous and was edible. I picked the fruit and ate it. It had a sharp, almost sour, but not unpleasant taste. It was like a lemon, but with a meatier texture.

I ate but didn't overdo it. I didn't want to end up with diarrhea, as I had not been eating fruit as regularly as I once did and knew the kind of reaction I might have due to a sudden diet of too much of it.

I walked on, and the land stayed damp for a great distance, but finally my feet were no longer sinking into the mud. I had lost the strands of cloth I had tied around my waist, and only the loin cloth I had made for myself remained. I am not particularly modest, having grown up among apes and having been naked for most of my early life, but I had learned to conceal my sex organs for those with more modest designs. As for the world in which I was now traveling, this was even less of a consideration than when I was with those who thought of themselves as civilized. But the cinching of the testicles was actually more comfortable than letting them swing free. I am well endowed. No brag, just fact.

I walked until the great mound of clay was in sight, the one I had seen from the height of the trees. The flood had washed into that area with a vengeance, but it had not done as great a damage as it had done to the terrain that lay behind me. There was a village just outside where the jungle rose up, and there were huts and villagers. The ground was wet, but not washed away. The villagers were dark of skin and lean of build and had painted their faces and naked buttocks with red ocher and white clay. They came out of their huts as I arrived. There were a lot of them. I raised my hands with the palms out, the universal sign of peace.

In response, they yelled and rushed me, brandishing clubs.

Perhaps they blamed me for the flood.

Seven

I had experienced a busy day.

I had fallen out of the sky in a zeppelin, swam for a long time and then floated in the burning heat on a bloated beast. I had swum again, and I had managed to make the shore and finally the jungle. I had climbed trees and endured a flood and lost a friend, and then I had walked a goodly distance, and now I was being attacked, though I no longer had as much as a sharp stick.

There was no reasoning with them. They yelled and I understood what they said. This was before Wells's injection, of course, but I found their language to be quite similar to that of the primates that had raised me.

They were saying "Capture him!"

It might have been best for them, even tired as I was, if they had tried to kill me, for trying to capture me limited them. I was not limited. I grabbed them and threw them and twisted their heads until their necks cracked like chicken bones in a wolf's mouth. I even ripped arms, not only out of their sockets, but tore them off, and used an arm in either hand as a weapon. I swung them and hit my new enemies and cracked skulls and shattered ribs, and still they came, like ants on a corpse, and finally they swarmed me.

I was very weak at this point, and could not even escape them to run away. They bore me down and stuck me with clubs and finally I passed out.

Eight

When I awoke I was tied to the mound as you found me. The villagers stood over me chanting. I understood their invocations. They were calling on the gods to send messengers from the sky to tear me apart, consume me, and guarantee better crops and calmer winds and a less wet world. My thought that they might have blamed me for the flood might have been more relevant than I first expected.

The one who I thought of as the priest held a long stick from which dangled colorful tufts of feathers. He struck me with the stick, and then they all went away.

I saw that there were burning bodies near me. There were a few that were still alive. I understood that I was a sacrifice. I feared I would be set afire, but noted that the bodies that were burning, and some were still alive, were ripped up and the fires had been built at a later time, after the wounds had been made. The fires had been built into the wounds. There were moaning dying men and women of all hues of skin and appearance.

I wondered what caused the wounds, but that was soon solved by the arrival of the birds, large and circling above, lowering themselves toward their offered meal. As I have mentioned, the same ones that had thought to make Leo and me their meal when we were floating on the creature raft.

I thought of Prometheus on his rock, of the great bird that tore out his liver on a daily basis, only to have it grow back so he would have to endure the painful process again and again.

In this case, it was a process one only experienced once, though I was certain that the actual event, and the pain that went with it, would seem to continue for all eternity.

Death would be a happy privilege.

I was considering on this as the birds gathered in greater numbers and began to descend. I had managed to pull one of the pegs from the clay. Actually, I had flexed enough to snap it off, as it was a long pole buried deep. Though I was exhausted, and only a partial version of the man I normally was, there was enough in me to manage that feat. Probably the peg, or pole, was aged and had been tugged on by many a hopeful survivor, weakening it over time. I try to be modest when it is called for. As I said, I was weak, so let me give some credence to the weakened pole point of view.

Whatever the reason, I freed a hand and was fighting the birds with it, and then Bill, the seal, and Wells showed up.

Thank goodness.

I was used to doing the rescuing, but certainly had no reservations about being rescued myself. I rested with them, ate, and continued.

And that is how I came to be where I was, traveling through the jungle, heading toward the mountains so that I might cross them and take hold of the Golden Fleece and bring it back to Jill.

Another Sneak Peek at Other Goings-On

SHE WHO MUST BE OBEYED AND EATS LUNCH EARLY had strange dreams inside her tent, which was of an enormous size and made of slave skin, sticks and bones. She was sitting, not lying, dark-dreaming on her throne, and in her dreams earth and bones were cracking beneath her, the trees going down under the weight of great machines, smoke rising up from their cremated ruins.

The dreams seemed real and false simultaneously. She knew who she was, and then she didn't. Her skull throbbed, and she could feel her brain move about inside of it as if seeking an exit. Alien minds flowed through her gray matter like water through cheese cloth. Their alien memories of weird worlds and events were now her memories, and those of her own life were mixed in and impossible to separate. She was Tomi and she was no longer Tomi.

She thought, I want to make greenery brown, make the seas dry up. I want the world flat and coated in paving stone and the flesh and bones of all who resist, and some that don't. I want my disappointment on dull parade, for I am me and them, and all of us are unhappy, so spread it around.

Then she was pulled out of her dream when her personal aide, General Joog, entered her tent. She sensed him before he was there. She had given him his title of General. Someday she would tire of him and eat him.

She called his name inside her head and he heard her inside his head. It was as if a talking darkness had moved into his skull when her mind spoke to him; a damp darkness he could smell and feel, an ancient serpent was crawling over his moldy soul.

General Joog was tall and lean and sunburned easy, had a long lower jaw and a lip that curled back on one side of his mouth and showed his teeth. One eye was lower than the other. Genetics had not been kind to him.

Once, when the world was different, he had danced and joshed and fooled about for local kings and chieftains, wore stupid hats and funny clothes, made jokes at his own expense. Women feared him for his appearance and men made fun of him.

He went from small kingdom to small kingdom, from village to village, from tribe to tribe, and made his jokes and did his dances, twisted and hopped for food and drink. Went from one place to the other, like a fly gravitating to the sweetest honey, and now the worm had turned, and he had the largest pot of honey to himself. He was no longer the fool.

The slaves, the army of She Who Must Be Obeyed and Eats Lunch Early, were his to piss on, to make fun of. He was General Joog and he had power and enforcers to make sure he maintained it. He could have all the women he wanted, men for that matter. He rode them like ponies, and sometimes he slit their throats or broke their backs and left them to squirm in the dirt like grubs. He did it because he could. He had learned that from She Who Must Be Obeyed and Eats Lunch Early.

Inside his head, where she frequently dwelled, she touched things in there that gave him pain, or fear, or made him confused, and sometimes, they even made him ashamed. She also gave him pleasure, showed him little beautiful things from places unknown. And then she would come to him in a red dress and say call me Tomi, and then inside his head Tomi would touch him with her furry hand. Her touch could be warm, and it could be cold. Happy pain was fused with sad delight in that touch. She moved from room to room inside his head, rearranged the furniture, and all the while she called him General.

He had told her of the Golden Fleece, and how powerful the village was that had it, and how powerful she would be if she had it. He said this sort of thing often, but he did in fact think the land where the fleece was kept was a good land, and if she took that land, maybe she would let him have some of it that wasn't rolled dirty flat or smoky brown, for he knew it would be less than what it was

after they were there, but that was the price to pay to no longer be a jumping fool.

But a corner, that's all he wanted, a corner of land with a bevy of wenches and a dozen slaves and a handful of guards to call his own. Maybe a nice little home made of wood and stone, perhaps a palace would be nice, a high wall around it all, some soldiers on the ramparts.

As for She Who Must Be Obeyed and Eats Lunch Early, she read his thoughts even when he tried not to think them. She read them, and she thought: The Golden Fleece. I like that.

She opened her eyes.

"We have paused long enough, General Joog, set a course," she said, actually speaking.

As strange as it was to hear her in his mind, it was even stranger to hear her speak. Her mouth seemed full of syrup, and her words bubbled up through it.

"Of course, your majesty," he said with his mouth.

General Joog set a course. And when She Who Must Be Obeyed and Eats Lunch Early limped out of her tent into the Ever Sunlight, favoring the foot that had been deep in the mud when she was down in the sea, her throne was carried out behind her and taken up and fastened into place on her rolling machine by her slaves.

She climbed on it like a monstrous turd rolling uphill. She locked herself onto and into her throne with straps and contraptions, pushed her naked raw ass into place. She settled with a deep sigh and when she sighed her breath was foul and it was like a cloud in the air for a long, long time. Lightning moved behind her eyes. Thunder rumbled in her stomach. Her bones groaned. Her blood boiled and her flesh crawled. The fur on her skin stood out like porcupine quills, and then settled slowly into place.

General Joog gave the command. Whips cracked. Slaves moaned, the army marched. The machines rolled.

Roll on, roll on.

And inside her head: I am Daddy's little girl. I am the finest little girl that ever lived. I am She Who Must Be Obeyed and Eats Lunch Early, and I love me and me loves me back and I think Daddy must have loved me. In that moment, she was Tomi and Tomi alone, and for a while, the little, red, furry ape girl descended deeper and deeper into her memories, and as always, she finally found herself at the bottom of the deep blue sea, her foot caught up in prehistoric mud.

For that thought alone, her foot caught up and her body weaving in the ebb and flow of the sea, someone, something, the very earth and all that moved on it, would suffer.

One

Leo

When Leo awoke he felt as if he had been mauled by a bear.

He lay in the mud that had been pushed up into a copse of trees and had pushed him there with it. He lay there hoping all his parts were working.

After a bit, he wiggled his feet, and then moved his legs. Nothing fell off. He sat up, and except for a sensation of being one giant bruise, he was okay.

Finally, standing, looking about, he found that the flood had set him not only in a copse of trees, but had lifted him high up on a hill. The trees at the top were all the vegetation in immediate view, though in the distance he could see the blue-black shape of the jungle, and beyond that the rising rocks and forests of the distant mountains. Down the side of the hill was a hundred-foot drop. He walked around the hill and found this was the case on every side. To make matters worse, the route down was nothing but slick mud, and lots of it, and then there was standing water, though it was draining even as he looked at it.

He considered for quite some time, and then decided there was nothing for it but to go down the hill, taking his chance in the mud, which was flapping with fish and cluttered with dead animals. There were no limbs or roots, or anything that he could comfortably grab onto to make his way down. It would be slippy-slide all the way.

Leo looked about, and then began to peel the bark off a large tree. The bark was loosened from impact with jungle debris and raging flood, and Leo found he could skin it, like pulling the rubber loose from a tire. He was able to strip a large piece of it loose.

Pushing the sheet of bark to the edge of the hill, he sat down on it, grabbed the front of the bark. It was flexible enough that he could pull it back so that it became a kind of shield before him.

He took a deep breath, nudged the bark a little by bumping it with his ass and rocking back and forth.

Nothing happened.

Leo took a deep breath and bumped again, and the bark began to slide. Slowly at first, and then away it went, moving like a freight train, Leo clutching to the edge of the bent-over bark in a white-knuckle grip.

He screamed as he jetted down the hill.

It was a quick trip, and it ended when he lost control of the impromptu sled and was thrown clear of it. He went sliding over the mud, and then went down into it, up to his arms, and lay there trapped.

"Shit," Leo said to the sky.

———◆———

It took work, but Leo was gradually able to free himself from the deep muck, scramble to the surface of it, and not sink again. He slid down the rest of the hill on his ass and fetched up hard against a shattered tree at the bottom.

"Ouch," he said.

He lay there for a few moments, then worked his way to his feet and began to trudge onward. There was some mud and water there, but it was not deep. His bare feet sank into the lesser mud, but it was not uncomfortable. As long as he didn't step on something bad along the way he would be fine, and in time he would work his way onto more solid ground.

So far, so good.

Things were looking up, he thought. He would go to the mountains and over the other side. It would take some time, but if Jack had survived, and it was his guess he had, as he always seemed to, he would be seeking Rumwara and the fleece. Perhaps he could catch up with him. Of course, he had no idea which route Jack had taken, and no idea where Rumwara actually was located.

Still, it was some kind of plan.

Two

Leo began to make his way toward the mountains. He stopped to sleep when he felt he had to and ate what he could find, which was mostly fruit and nuts and tubers. It was a sparse diet and he was always hungry and the diet gave him the shits.

He could only guess how long it would take him to accomplish his trip to the mountains, but they were growing closer. Time in Down World was impossible to judge accurately, though if Jack were here he'd have a decent idea of how long he had traveled; he had an internal clock. He was the kind of guy could tell you how far something was by looking and could hear a rabbit hop across the ground during deep sleep.

Leo was making his way down a forested trail, carrying a heavy limb for a club, when he heard a noise of rattles and bangs and clangs and screeches, and all manner of business.

He saw trees toppling in the distance, splits of light shining through the forest. And then he saw a great machine made of stone and metal and sitting atop that machine was a mass of meat with red fur covering it, and even from a distance he could tell that what he was looking at wasn't exactly human. It was a huge hairball and there were warriors in light leather armor and caps all around the machine that was being pulled by a row of slaves. Whips cracked, words snapped.

Unlike the others, Leo had not received the language serum, but he understood the drift. The slaves were being encouraged, to use a polite word, to pull. As the machine dragged out of sight, Leo saw there were other machines, smaller and light-looking, and there were rows and rows of slaves. There were warriors in all manner of martial dress, carrying mostly spears, some bows and arrows, but on their hips were swords, and in their belts were sling shots that could be whirled about their heads to release stones, most likely contained in the bags that hung from their belts.

Leo began to step backwards, trying to return to the forest, but then a soldier looked up, cried out, and pointed at him.

The shit had hit the fan.

They came en masse, and Leo knew there was no way he could outrun them. They came in a horde of voices and raised weapons. The first few that came near were hit with his club. Skulls were cracked, arm and leg bones were broken, but still they came. So many.

And then a sling shot was spun over one of the soldier's heads, and a stone was released. It hit the club Leo was brandishing, bounced off and hit him between the eyes and knocked him on his ass and out.

Three

When Leo came awake his wrists were tied with ropes and he was being dragged on his belly toward the mass of men and women, and even children. His forehead hurt where the rock had struck him. He was kicked, and finally pulled to his feet.

He knew what was in store for him immediately.

He was put in a spot near the front, probably because he was strong, fresh meat not yet worn down completely. It was painful work, and even his fresher muscles ached immediately and a feeling of despair washed over him and into him. As time wore on, it only became darker and more hopeless in feeling, and he thought that, as he had seen some do, he would throw himself under the grinding wheels and make his way to death's door.

But he couldn't do it.

It wasn't in him.

He breathed. He lived. And though this was not a life worth breathing, where there was a will there might be a way, and an escape.

Leo struggled in the harness that was attached to him, that bit into his skin, and it was as if he felt the struggles of all his distant ancestors, laboring against their will, told by others they were inferior to justify their inhumanity to man. It was a feeling of weight and despair.

The slaves were moved to the back of the machines when the jungle showed up, and there, with long thick poles, they pushed, made the machines roll, crunch against the tree trunks, taking them down, grinding them under. Strange beasts and creatures were used as well for pushing and pulling. They bled and moaned like the humans moaned.

Whips cracked. Backs bled and burned as if set on fire.

Leo dreamed of taking a whip away from the main man, the one he had heard called Joog. An ugly, tall, sun-red man with mean black eyes and a shaved head.

I want to kill him, Leo thought. I want to take him in my hands and snap his neck like a chicken bone.

When the trail ahead opened up naturally, the slaves were whipped harder. The lash burned into his back and the sweat and blood ran down his body.

Leo lifted his head and looked out toward the cool blue mountains beyond.

One

From the Journal of Ned the Seal

I HATE EVERYBODY.

I actually wrote that on my slate. I don't know why, but I did. I think right then I did hate everyone. I wanted to go back to Time Machine. I wanted to rest. I wanted some hot chocolate made by Clarence. I wanted to pull my little weiner. I wanted my old routine.

Again, it was hard to accept, but I was tired of adventures.

And, I was lost. After being pursued by dinosaurs and odd-looking natives with tails, I realized that if I tried to reenter the jungle and find the old path, I was more likely to be lost worse, or eaten by some monster.

I thought about where Jack and Bill and Suzie Q said they were going. Beyond the mountains where the Golden Fleece was. Maybe I should go that way.

Maybe I shouldn't.

It was really a flip a coin decision. I didn't have a coin. I thought on it for about a minute. The mountains were a sure thing to go to. I couldn't tell directions otherwise. The jungle was on all sides of the river, thick and green and full of howling beasts. The river had beasts as well, but it was a clearer highway. That was the thing to do. Head down the river toward the mountains.

I could also go back down the river, but then again, I wasn't sure where that led and the current would be a fight by boat. I didn't want to swim either. Lots of monsters in that water, and I'd have to give up my sled and my new horn. The only thing that seemed like a good idea was going where Tango was going. He knew stuff. I decided that's what I'd do.

Maybe I could find reason to honk my horn.

Of course, I could.

Two

And so, Gentle Reader, Ned, the Intrepid Seal, set out on a great adventure he didn't want to undertake, but what choice did he have?

How had his life come to this?

Did he not deserve better?

Would he prevail?

Was it not sad he had to leave his fez on the sled so as not to lose it? He looked so snappy and masculine when he had it on.

A lot of female seals, if he were to cross paths with them, would tell him so. He didn't cross paths with any, however.

Now, all he had was river and jungle, and far and away, the sight of the mountains.

<hr>

Okay.

That was me writing about myself. I want to write Dime Novels and such. I like to practice from time to time. I have a little journal I keep, a diary, on board my sled. It gives me comfort to write in it. I want to go back to the world and era of Dime Novels. I want to write adventures about my adventures and I want to make up new adventures and not have adventures anymore.

Enough is enough.

Well, almost. There were still things to come.

<hr>

The river was long, and in some places quite wide and in others so narrow you could reach out on one side with a paddle and touch the shore, and then do the same on the opposite side. It had both deep and shallow sections and there were places where the water ran swift, and others where it ran slow. I was tempted to leave the boat and take to my sled, but I thought it best to conserve my battery power. I didn't want to be caught with my pants down, if I had worn pants, while charging up the sled, and then have no way to exit as quickly as I would like. The sled would work all the time, but not as well when it was battery weak. When it was really weak, a turtle could outrun it. When it was well charged a cheetah couldn't catch it.

Down the river I went, letting the current carry me for the most part, but keeping the boat on track by dipping a paddle now and then at the back of the boat, using it as a crude rudder.

I swam in the river from time to time, caught fish to eat, and then I would climb back in the boat and drift along. Now and again I went ashore. I had a lot of modifications, thanks originally to Doctor Momo and later H. G. Wells, and one of them was I could do without being in water for long periods. It's a modification in the brain, and I was glad to have it. The device attached to my skull that enhanced my brain was waterproof, and not so large that I was aware of it anymore. If I wanted, I could cover it with my fez.

For now, I kept the fez in a pouch on my sled, which rested in the middle of the boat, but when the day grew hot, I would put it on to keep the brain enhancer, as I called it, from heating up too much. Sometimes it could become quite warm and make me think my brain was being fried for breakfast. I also had gained a lot of dexterity with my oversized thumbs grafted to my flippers. Doctor Momo used to say about my thumbs that they were as handy as a pocket on a shirt. Momo didn't turn out to be a good man, by the way, and I don't have a shirt. But the thumbs are nice.

I don't know how long I sailed in the boat, ate fish from the river, or ventured on shore now again to look for fruit, or to break the boredom, but it was a long time. Sometimes I had to go on shore because black clouds brought howling wind and blowing rain, storms and floods. I would pull the boat into a little cove or indention in the river, and then I would use my sled to find some place under the trees. There was a tarp I could pull up from the front of the sled, and it would drape completely over and make a kind of tent. It was surprisingly comfortable and dry. But the problem was, on shore, I had to watch for even more problems in the form of hungry creatures who would have loved a seal for a meal.

I know I have said all this, but you have to understand how important these thoughts were to me.

Once, when the air was clear and the sun was hot, I sailed by a place where there was a bleak stretch of land, and I could see smoke puffing up from big black pits. This went on for miles, and while I was scratching my head (actually my butt), I encountered another mystery. Great balls of something or another, floating high in the sky. I fetched my eye glass stored on the sled and pointed it toward them and took a gander.

Turned out they were thin transparent balls with plantlike tendrils hanging from them. On some, birds were taking a ride. I even saw a squirrel on one. I don't know if it had been the squirrel's intent to ride on the floating ball, but there he was, blowing onward toward the Blue Mountains, looking a little agitated. If I could have given him advice, it would have been not to dig too deep with its claws. That might lead to serious problems.

Finally, I saw where the balls had come from. They floated up from the limbs of trees, like giant chunks of clear pollen came loose, naturally I presumed, and floated up and away, spreading the tree's seed. I had never seen trees like that, transparent seeds like that.

And then the trees were falling. I could see the taller trees going down beyond a stretch of undamaged trees, and the balls were coming loose of the trees and shooting upward into the sky. I could hear the trees crack, and down they went, and I heard a rumbling noise that I finally decided was a multitude of voices. There was also the sound of something clunking and clanking. Lots of somethings actually.

I paddled close to shore and let the boat drift slow alongside a rise of high water-weeds and cane. I grabbed at the cane and made the boat stop. I fastened a rope to a clutch of cane and used that as a moor line.

Then I eased over the side of the boat and wormed my way through the water-weeds until I was close to shore and could stick my nose through the vegetation.

The jungle fell. The balls went up and high and there were so many they decorated the sky. The earth trembled, and on they came, for miles and miles.

People.

Machines.

There was one great machine in front of them all. Its grinding wheels were propelled by pushing and pulling slaves. Following behind it, and beside it, were thousands of other slaves, bringing along smaller machines.

There were warriors too. Of all skin colors and type of dress. Some wore only tunics, others wore leather armor and carried wicker shields. They all carried weapons. Bows and arrows, swords and clubs, slings, and spears, mostly spears. They marched steadily. The machines appeared to be siege engines, or maybe just war machines. They were enormous in size, but one was larger than all the others. They could be pushed or pulled and at that moment it was both. Slaves in straps tugged it along, and at the backs of them slaves pushed with large poles with a series of grips along their path, each grip spot stationed by a slave.

There were wagons drawn by oxen and beasts I had never seen before, lizard creatures the size of horses, strapped in harness, beat and poked and hastened onward.

They passed beside those smoking black pits. And finally, they stopped. The front and largest machine was wheeled around and pushed and pulled closer to one of the pits. That's when I saw something large and covered in red fur sitting on a throne at the highest point of the machine. Due to the sagging breasts and the spread legs, relaxed and short on modesty, I determined that I was looking at a giant female. She was bulbous in shape and the shape swelled and moved. It looked like something nervous was inside of her, something large. Her mouth hung open and smoke rolled out of it. Electricity crackled around her head like a colorful wreath.

The army and the slaves were stopped in their tracks, and except for a handful of warriors and the slaves that operated the Big One's machine, the rest stayed back in the distance.

The Big One studied the smoking pits for a long time, turning her head slowly from left to right, as if it wasn't fastened on very well.

Then she called out, "General Joog."

What an odd voice. All gurgle and glue.

A man grabbed a ladder on the side of the machine, hustled up it and leaned toward her. I saw his body tremble. He might be in her service, but he feared her. I could smell his fear from where I hid at the edge of the bank, my nose poking through a concealment of weeds. Her mouth didn't move, but he seemed to be taking in information, nodding along. Telepathy. I knew that's what it was. I'm a smart seal. She was no longer speaking the words, she was sending them.

Moments later the man came down. He shouted some orders I couldn't quite hear, and then whips cracked and slaves moaned. I saw one black man, black as my seal hide, look at the one called General Joog with such intensity I could feel it all the way where I hid amongst the grass and cane. The man wore tattered clothes, and they looked like clothes from Above World, or Up World, whatever it was that Tango called it. He was big and strong and had an attitude, even though whips wrapped around his shoulders and the blunt ends of spears poked him. I recognize attitude, because I have one.

I lay there for a long time and watched great cauldrons being brought to the pits. They had crafted long handles from felled tree limbs, and they used those to rig devices to attach to the cauldrons and dip out the smoking blackness, which I could now see was an oily, smoldering tar. One man slipped at the edge of one of the pits and his leg went in.

He yelled and the big black man pulled him out. The man's leg was gone. There was only steaming bone where it had been. Soldiers ran forward and grabbed the black man and pulled him back, popped him with whips, then they flung the injured man into the boiling tar, laughing as they did. I suppose they saw it as a wise move. It wasn't like they were going to nurse him, whereas the black man was still a strong worker. The injured man landed in the tar and went under fast with a puff of smoke. He didn't have time to yell again.

They dipped the tar and loaded it in huge black pots and wooden crates that steamed and leaked the mess. It was all put on flatbed wagons, and then slats were placed on the sides and the ends of the great wagons, and after enough had been loaded, or perhaps all their receptacles had been filled, the wagons moved on. The whole army moved, the machine with the furry red blob on the throne was rolled to the front of the horde.

I watched for what seemed like forever as the army traveled along. It was a lot of army. Or rather there were a lot of slaves and enough of an army; far more slaves than army. But the army was armed and the slaves were not.

When they came to the jungle the slaves in front, the ones pulling, went to the rear and helped the others push. Against the jungle they went. Trees cracked and fell and were rolled under the great wheels of the machine, followed by the slaves, the army, more machines, and wagons. Fire were set amongst the trees for no good reason. The downed forest flamed and smoked, and the army rolled on.

I didn't move from my position until the machines and slaves and army were out of sight, traveling toward the Blue Mountains. Their progress went on for a long time. Whiffs of black smoke from the steaming pots of tar went with them. The whole thing made me shiver. Humans. They were hard to figure.

I returned to the boat. I sailed past a number of small outlets in the river, creeks and side streams, but I stayed on the main river. It was no longer flowing directly toward the Blue Mountains, but I hoped it would soon loop in that direction once again. If not, then I might have to take to my sled and try to make my way there, avoiding that massive army. Thinking about that monster on the throne, all those poor slaves, and the army itself, gave me the willies.

I was considering on all of this when I made the wide bend in the river and saw a lot of little boats coming my way. The boats were packed with naked, skinny, red-skinned people and the people and boats were draped with blue and white flowers the size of elephant heads. They were singing, and it was very melodious singing.

Lying on a slanting platform in the foremost boat, near the front of it like a figurehead on the bow of a sailing ship, was a man. I could tell who it was immediately, he was so tall and broad of shoulder.

He had a blood-stained bandage of some kind on his head. He wore nothing but the sunlight on his skin and his skin glistened from his sweat. He wasn't moving. His eyes appeared closed. It was Tango.

There was nothing I could do to avoid them. They surprised me, and before I knew it, I was sailing in their midst, passing the boat Tango was in, ending up with boats on either side of me.

I grabbed my shock rod, as I am now calling it, and leaped... Well, I kind of waddled quickly into the water and then into the boat carrying Tango, and I stuck the rod against one of the red-skinned women's ankle.

Boy did she jump.

Right out of the boat.

And then the red men and women were on me.

"Stop it! Please. He is my friend."

It was Tango. He was standing in the boat now, off the platform, smiling at me.

The red people backed off. But not before a little girl kicked me in the side. I might have hit her with the shock rod a little.

Okay. I did. She jumped and screamed.

"That's enough, Ned," Tango said. "Please, friends, forgive him. He thought he was rescuing me."

One of the women laughed. "He doesn't look like much of a rescuer," she said. "He is plump, though."

"Don't underestimate him," Tango said. "My belief is he's quite resourceful."

I took hold of the slate around my neck and used my grease pencil to write. I THOUGHT YOU WERE A CAPTIVE.

"No, they rescued me after I helped them, and they are taking me to their village to feed me. I have to attend a feast. Sort of mandatory. I thought you went back to Time Machine."

I wiped my previous remarks clear of the slate with my flipper, wrote, I GOT LOST.

Three

The folk accepted me kindly and gave me some fruit to eat. It was a big yellow fruit and it smelled like someone's nasty ass, and it didn't taste much better, but I was hungry and I ate it quickly, glad to have it, hoping at the same time I would never have to eat it again.

As I ate, I looked about, saw that one of the boats was nearly filled with dead people, and only one living human, a long, lean woman with a bleeding bald patch on her head that suggested hair had been ripped out in a fight, was in it.

What it turned out, according to Tango, was that he was a hero, and that was why he was being celebrated with flowers and song and a sweet boat ride on the platform, absorbing the rays of the internal sun. I already knew he was a hero. But what he meant was he was a hero again, therefore the celebration. He didn't mind telling me he was a hero, but as he accurately reminded me, if it's true, it's not blowing hot smoke up your ass. It's telling it like it is.

This is his story, and pardon me if I try and capture some of Tango's poetic expression, but I pride myself, as a would-be Dime Novelist, on being able to imitate the spirit of others words, even if they are my words.

Something like that.

Here goes:

After Tango left us and I started back to Time Machine, he lost contact with Bill and Suzie Q, and had gone far by passage through the trees (that's how he put it, by passage through the trees) when he came upon the rat-people, light of bones, scuttling through the forest on all fours, climbing trees and leaping about swift as monkeys. They were a gray-white horde with human-like features, but with elongated snouts packed full of sharp rat teeth. Their beady black eyes looked like chunks of coal and their tails lifted in the wind and waved about like snakes rising from the grass. Tango saw them from some distance, coming through the jungle from the direction of the great Blue Mountains.

He was fortunately far enough away, and the wind was blowing in a safe direction, not carrying his scent to them. They gathered up in a massive tree in a wad of furry bodies. Tango assumed they must be preoccupied with prey below, and he decided to wait in the leafy shadows, let the ancient scenario of hunter and quarry play out, leaving him an escape point.

But the loose sphincter of life was waiting with a bowel full of shit.

A wind was howling down from a great dark shadow near the central sun; obviously a gap in the world that led to the outer crust. Miles and miles up it appeared nothing more than a smudgy spot.

The wind was not cold like the other winds, but hot, and it was filled with dark flakes that appeared to be ash, as if blown out from some kind of eruption. (I want to emphasize I've always said the sun was caused by volcanic activity.) The wind lifted the limbs and leaves of the trees and rattled them like maracas.

Tango thought he had it made in the shade. They would attack their prey below, and he would continue onward, avoiding them altogether.

However, that was when the sphincter of life I mentioned let loose.

En masse, the rat-people let out with chitters and little barks and down the trees they went, some leaping from great heights, spreading their arms, which Tango now saw had folds of skin like flying squirrels. The hot wind lifted them at first, and then they were dropped, gliding down on the shifting currents. Their chittering became an insane babble of hungry excitement, and when the tree cleared of them, Tango moved, but as he passed over where the rats had been, he saw a tableau (he used that word) below that caused him to pause and reconsider his exit.

The rat-people were so many that when they landed on their prey they appeared to foam like dark sea waves, and what they foamed over were human beings, the very ones that were now carrying us along in their boats. The skinny, red folk.

"Something inside of me," Tango said, "connected me to my tribe—humans, though on the whole I am not that proud of them and prefer to think of myself as coming from the apes who raised me. But when I saw those people fighting valiantly, and considered the hordes of rat-people, I pulled my knife, and foolishly descended."

Isn't that nice? Foolishly descended.

Into their midst Tango dropped, his knife flashed in one hand, and with the other he grabbed and punched and poked. He kicked out with both legs. He was bitten in spots and hit in the head by a falling rat-person (thus the later to be bandaged head wound), but on he fought, and the dead rat-people piled up around him like dog turds.

They were multitude, but they were easy to kill he said. One knife strike, one punch, one kick, flinging them hard against tree trunks, and they were off to the great Rat Hole in the sky.

The rats kept coming and Tango and the people on the ground kept fighting, working their way through a gap in the jungle toward the river. They had parked their boats there, had gone ashore to gather fruits.

The fight went on, and the rats were coming out of places where there didn't seem to be places. The people Tango was trying to save had clustered behind him, for it was obvious that he was the best of the fighters. They were backing toward the river, Tango at the front, but backing with them.

And still the creatures came.

There were children in the hunting party. Turned out that the tribe worked that way, carried every damn body with them on a hunt and gather, and one of them was a little girl, the very one that had kicked me. The tribe had pushed the children to the center as they fought the rat-people, but one of the creatures had wormed its way between the legs of the warriors and grabbed the child and pulled her back through a turmoil of thrashing limbs and dragged her out into the open. The rats swarmed her, and it would have been all over except for Tango.

"I moved quickly, little seal. I jumped into their midst, and by this point the blood lust was on me. It was fight or flight and flight was not my choice. I grabbed a rat thing by the tail and used him as a weapon. I pulled the girl—lightly nipped, but not badly injured—free of the rat pile and used the rat I had by the tail as a kind of mace. Its body had perfect balance and was easy to sling, considering I have extraordinary muscles.

"Sometimes, whatever is in me, whatever has shaped me, loses its civilized veneer, and all that is left is the savage. A dose of something even more powerful than adrenaline surges through me; the juice of the jungle, you might call it. All of those moments of growing up amongst the apes and becoming one of them, fighting creatures that should be stronger than me, but are not, due to my father's serum before the longevity drug I received. That drug that made me super-human, and sometimes when I'm angry, it surges inside of me and stews my innards and makes me a monster of rage."

PAUSE
At that point in Tango's story I wrote on my slate.
WAIT. YOU HAVE A SUPERHUMAN DRUG IN YOU?
"My very genetics have been changed, little seal. I am superhuman, but not invulnerable. Just stronger, quicker, and in some ways, smarter than the average human."
YOU DID NOT MENTION THIS BEFORE
"Isn't it obvious?"
TOUCHE

BACK TO THE RAT BATTLE
"I swung the rat and I kicked and bit and yelled my jungle yell, the one I had learned from the great apes that raised me. It was a reflex. A war cry. A death song. And only moments later I could hear something moving through the trees, and out of the corner of my eyes, I saw them.
"Ape-men."

One

Tango the Ape Man Tells it First Hand

They came along the ground, running on their knuckles, and they came rustling through the trees, leaping from limb to limb. They had black and gray fur and they were longer and leaner than gorillas, but had the same appearance of impossible strength; looked the way you might think of an Australopithecine Robustus looking, but larger and more powerful. Of course, you may not think about an Australopithecine at all, but that's the best I can do.

They collided with the mass of rat-people, and like me they were grabbing them and flinging them, using them for weapons in the same way I was. The rat-people clawed at me, tore off my loin cloth in their attempt to take me down.

I continued to swing the dead rat-man, its body becoming flatter and messier with each blow. And then the rat-people scampered, dissolved into the jungle as quickly as they had appeared, leaving only a few fading squeaks and a lot of corpses and rat turds behind them as they went.

I let loose of the dead rat creature's tail, let it drop onto the mulchy ground with a damp splat.

The jungle ceased to rattle and crunch with the rat-people's retreat. The warm wind gently moved the trees. The apes turned and looked at me. One of them, a large female, moved close, stuck her face close to mine to show she was without fear.

"You knew our cry?" she said to me. Had I not had the device inside of me, I would have still understood them perfectly; except for a slight accent they spoke the language of the apes who raised me, and I use the term ape for simplification. It is my belief they are far closer to humans than apes.

Several of them, males and females, came cautiously forward and sniffed me. I didn't make any sudden moves. I was as strong as any one of them, but not any two of them. They sniffed my face, my ass and balls.

"I am of your people. The tribe of Morhana from the great world above," I said.

"That shit hole," the she-ape said. "It is horrible up there. I do not know your tribe. And where is your hair?"

"They are much like you," I said. "Our war cry is the same. And I was raised by the Morhana, but I am human."

The she-ape was looking around at the crowd of humans I had helped. Some of them were dead on the ground, women and children. The tribe of humans were starting to pick them up and carry them through the jungle toward the river.

"May we not have the dead ones to eat?" Said the she-ape. "The rat things taste awful. Stringy."

"No. These people have their rituals and feelings same as you."

The she-ape sniffed loudly. "But they are not apes."

"Still, it's the same. Am I not human? Am I not discussing with you in the language of our ancestors?"

"That does not make you the same as us."

That hurt, I must admit.

"I suppose that is true, but I was raised on the milk of the Morhana, a lovely ape named Fra, and she was my mother."

The she-ape studied me closely. All the apes did. They were sniffing me from the feet up still. The tribe of humans, besides those that had carried the bodies away, stood ready with their simple weapons, waiting, not knowing what to expect. I could have told them that if the apes decided to fight them, they might as well bend over and kiss their asses goodbye.

"You called, we answered," said the she-ape.

"It was a habit, my war cry," I said, "but I am grateful brothers and sisters."

"Cousins," said the she-ape. "Distant cousins. Most likely, very distant."

"Very well, distant cousin. I much appreciate your help. I have no offerings other than my thanks for your help."

"I would have liked fruit, or maybe the bodies of the humans. The rat-people can rot."

"Then rot they shall," I said.

The she-ape was quiet for a long time. "If you need your family, for we are your family if you were raised by our kind, and from your actions it seems you were, then call on us. We live beyond here, toward the mountains, near the river shore. I am Rotah."

"Tango," I said.

"Ah, a good name. We know of you. We have heard of you. We have heard of you from ancestors who came down here from up there, through a hole in the world. Your legend is ripe and you have lived long."

In ape language calling something ripe was good.

"You are my sister," I said.

She thought on that a moment, realizing I had moved our relations closer.

"You are my cousin," she said, and we embraced and all the apes of her tribe hopped up and down and grunted and hooted and beat their chests with acceptance. A couple of the males masturbated rapidly. To be polite, I did the same. I didn't want them to think I didn't enjoy the same simple things in life that they did. As I did, the human tribe watched me with amazement, but no one said a thing, and they let me finish. It was satisfying, and a cultural necessity.

Really. It was.

A moment later the apes faded into the jungle.

Two

The humans called themselves the Ones, and they led me to the river and to their boats, the manner by which they had arrived at the edge of the jungle. We stopped on the shore as everyone bandaged and treated wounds with jungle remedies. They had come here to gather nuts and fruits, and then, the rat-people came. Now they had decided it was best to get back on the river and head home, even if they were mostly empty-handed.

I would have thought they would have wanted to hunt and gather, but the rat-people had taken the wind out of them.

The women, and this wasn't a half-bad situation, rubbed a salve all over my body. It smelled sweet and tangy at the same time. They bandaged my head and put me in a position of honor at the front of one of their boats, gathered flowers and sang songs of my bravery and of our fight with the rat-people, of the great apes who came to help, and how the apes treated me with honor and respect, and how when I masturbated I gave up great white wads of sperm. The Ones then took turns and spoke highly of me, of my great prowess and courage, which I think is an accurate depiction.

Then along came Ned. I was so glad to see that little seal. I had a brief acquaintance with him, but there was something noble about the little guy, and he was certainly brave, attacking my adopted tribe before he understood I was not a captive. It was great to now have him as a companion along with the Ones, my adoptive tribe. Though, a reassessment of that adoption would be soon in the making.

As we moved along the river, I looked over at Ned in his boat. It had been fastened to the one I was in, and now that the situation was clear in Ned's mind, he knew we were safe, he had crawled into the comfort of his sled and pulled a little tarp over the device. I could hear him snoring.

Along the river we went, and finally off of the main stretch and down a narrow waterway that was easy to miss, so overhung was the entrance to it by drooping vines and moss.

The Ones stood up in their boats and parted the moss and vines gently and our boat sailed through them. Behind those vines there was a dark and narrow stretch of water, and then the light came through thinning trees, and finally the water opened out into a wide sun-sparkled lake. The lake was surrounded by a village full of simple cone-shaped huts, and the dense jungle nearly surrounded the lake.

At the edge of the lake was a moss-covered paddle wheel, a steamboat that could only have come from the surface world.

Ned had awakened by this point, removed his tarp tent and rolled it up with his little flippers and grafted thumbs. He was quite dexterous with those things, I should add.

Ned looked at the paddle wheel. His mouth fell open.

He wrote on his pad: HOLY SHIT. MARK TWAIN WOULD LOVE THIS.

Three

It was a large paddle wheel and looked in fair shape from where we were. It was docked near the shore in the little cove. I didn't try to have a look up close right away, as I didn't want to take away from the spirit of friendship I was sharing with the Ones.

Ned, on the other hand, dove into the water and went to the paddle wheel immediately.

When all the boats were on shore and we had stepped off of them, I spoke to the leader of the Ones about the paddle wheel. He was calls Tus.

"It came floating down the river with dead people on board. We ate them."

"Oh."

"They hadn't been dead long, so it wasn't nasty."

"I see."

Okay. Maybe I had been a hero, but it suddenly occurred to me that a lot of what had been rubbed into my body might have been something other than salve. The smell of it reminded me of a number of dinner herbs, now that I considered. In some cultures, the brave amongst a group were sacrificed, and sometimes eaten. Seals were eaten as a matter of course. I became cautious. I noticed how the Ones were looking at me. It was the same sort of admiration reserved for a nice cut of meat.

From that point on, I was cautious, and had begun to think I should have moved on and let the attack on them by the rat-people play out in natural course.

I pressed on about the paddle wheel.

"It showed up one day. Came from the river and ended up here. It made a noise as it came. It beat at the water with the wooden paddles.

It stopped here and went silent. We eventually went on board. There were dead men on the boat. One was extremely fresh. He had died shortly after he came to our lake. He had found our village by accident, is my guess. He had a lot of hair on his face, more than you have. But it didn't hurt the taste. It burned off in the fire."

It was true my beard had grown out a bit. I usually shaved it with my knife on a daily basis, but I had been so desperate to reach the Golden Fleece, I hadn't bothered. I knew that my beard at this point would be like golden peach fuzz. It grew slow and soft and was easy to shave.

I noticed Tus was eyeing me again, and I had that same feeling as before, as if I were a nice cut of meat. Everyone in this world seemed anxious to eat someone else. I suppose you took your meals where you could find them in Under World.

"Speaking of food," I said, "perhaps there is something for me and my friend, Ned, to eat, and then if there are no objections, I would enjoy looking over that boat. Where I come from, those were once prominent means of transportation. That was long ago, though."

"No shit?"

"No shit."

Ned finally showed up on the deck of the paddle wheel. He had what looked like a book in his mouth. He leapt gently from the deck and into the water, keeping his head up to keep the book from becoming soaked.

When he finally swam to shore and waddled over, he poked his nose and the book at me. I took it. Flipped it open. It was a diary.

"What is that?" said Tus.

"A diary," I said.

"What is that?"

"A person's thoughts recorded on paper."

He gently took the book from me and opened it. "What do these marks mean?"

I realized then that this tribe of friendly, perhaps hungry, folk didn't have a concept of writing.

"They are like bugs," Tus said, touching the writing.

"Indeed, they are. Talking bugs."

Tus gave me a quizzical grin.

"Perhaps I can explain it to you later."

Tus nodded and handed me back the diary.

"Let's get your sled," I said to Ned, and we hustled off to do that without discussing it with the tribe.

When we came to the boat where Ned's sled was, he wrote on his pad. I READ SOME OF THE DIARY. THEY ARE FROM ABOVE. THEY FOUND A WATER PATH DOWN UNDER. THERE WAS A GREAT STORM.

Ned paused to wipe the board clean.

THEY WERE SUCKED INTO WHAT THE CAPTAIN DESCRIBED AS A VORTEX OF WATER. THE WATER OPENED UP AND PULLED THEM DOWN.

He cleaned the tablet and wrote again.

THE VORTEX WAS DRY IN THE CENTER. THE WALLS WERE WATER. IT SPUN DOWN INSIDE THE EARTH AND PUKED THEM IN THE RIVER.

He wiped the slate again and wrote.

THE BOAT ENDED UP HERE.

He cleaned the slate again.

THE SAILORS LIVED IN THE BOAT FOR A TIME. THEN THEY MADE CONTACT WITH THE TRIBE. IT WAS NOT GOOD CONTACT.

Ned used his flipper to wipe the slate.

ONE OF THE MEN WENT OUT TO VISIT WITH THE TRIBE. THEY ATE HIM. THERE WERE FOUR ON BOARD. THEY BARRICADED THEMSELVES IN THE BOAT AND TRIED TO SAIL AWAY.

Wipe.

THE TRIBE BLOCKED THE MOUTH OF THE RIVER WITH LOGS. THEY COULDN'T GET OUT. THAT WAS THE LAST ENTRY. I CAN GUESS THE REST OF IT.

"Me too," I said.

This wasn't exactly the story Tus had told me. It sounded like they had killed the men for food, not merely eaten a dead body. I should make a note of clarity here. Once, lost in the Himalayas, trekking in search of the Abominable Snowman, as the beast is sometimes called, the expedition I was leading became trapped by snow and ice, and one of our Sherpas died. Rations were low, so we ended up eating him. He cooked out stringy and tough, but unlike the stories you hear about how human meat taste like pork, it was much more akin to beef. I could see how one might develop a taste for it. Later we encountered the Abominable Snowman. They cook out well and taste like yak.

Ned was writing again.

THE BOAT WAS A TOURIST BOAT OUT OF NEW ORLEANS. THEY GOT CAUGHT UP IN THAT WEIRD STORM THAT SUCKED THEM DOWN INTO THIS WORLD.

"And then, suddenly, they were tourist on their own tourists boat. Here's some news for you, Ned. The leader of the tribe said they were dead when the boat arrived."

I DON'T BELIEVE THAT.

"Neither do I. I may have helped a tribe survive an attack, only to have them plan to cook us up with a few wild vegetables."

US?

"Of course, plump little seal."

HEY, I HAVE BEEN WORKING OUT. A LITTLE. SOMETIMES. OKAY. NOT THAT MUCH.

"A warning. Watch your fat ass."

AND A PLEASANT WATCH IT WILL BE. NOT TO GO ALL HUMAN ON YOU AND STUFF, BUT MAYBE YOU SHOULD GET LIKE A JOCK STRAP OR SOMETHING. YOUR BUSINESS IS HANGING OUT, AND I'M SHORT, SO...

"I get your meaning," I said.

Four

When we joined the tribe, me walking, Ned on his sled, they were building a large fire. There were a lot of weapons at ready. There were not only the people I had encountered in the jungle, that I had saved from the rat-people, there were others I had not seen before. They were all a lean-looking bunch, and the awareness of that doubled my concerns. Perhaps had they been more successful in their hunting and gathering and had been willing to consume the rat-people, the situation might have been different. Nobody, from the apes to them, appeared to care for the rats, though.

I said to one of the women, a fine-looking specimen wearing a ship captain's hat, more likely the steamboat captain's hat, "Are you having a cookout?"

"Why yes. We are. You two are our guests of honor."

"I thought we might be," I said. "Well, while you are preparing the fire, we are going to take a look at the big boat."

Tus appeared out of nowhere.

"Do not go far. We hope to have the fire built up high soon. Then the meat goes on it. You should be here for that."

"Where's the meat?" I asked.

Tus cleared his throat.

"I suppose you could say it's in storage."

I couldn't help myself. "Is it good meat?"

"Perhaps a little tough, but I believe it will be flavorful."

"I see."

He eyed Ned.

"But, we have another large cut of meat that is fattier and should mix well. We have tubers to bake too."

"I do love tubers."

"Who doesn't?"

"We are going to look on the boat now," I said. "We will be right back."

RIGHT BACK, Ned wrote on his slate.

We went away from there, away from the heat of the fire. For now, the pile of wood and the rise of flames was high and hot and the smoke was thick and white. I assume their plan was to take me by surprise, and from behind, perhaps get me plastered on some sort of grog first. Obviously, they knew they couldn't take me in a fight. They knew a lot of them working together couldn't take me in a fight. They had seen me at work on the rat-people. Subterfuge would be their plan.

As we went, Ned clutched his shock rod, and kept looking over his shoulder.

We arrived at the boat. Ned glided his sled over the water. I swam. I pulled myself up on the boat by a dangling rope, and then Ned rose his sled up and I helped him and his device onto the deck.

Inside the wheelhouse, I looked around as Ned sledded into the room behind me.

I laughed a little. There was a gas gauge. I thumped it with my finger. It didn't move from its level, which was nearly full. I looked and saw there was a key in an ignition.

"It's motorized," I said. "It's a complete tourist sham."

It was obvious that this was indeed a tourist rental boat. It may have had a paddle wheel, and it even had a smoke stack, a steam setup, but it operated primarily on gasoline. It appeared the workers on the boat ended up caught in a strange whirlpool before they loaded guests.

Down World seemed to be full of holes. Entry points. And one of them had opened up and sucked them down, and somehow, perhaps through seismic shift, sealed itself off again, marooning them here on the river. They had to have seen the moss and the little tributary and thought there might be a place to hole up. Perhaps they had already had unpleasant encounters, but due to the fullness of the gas tank, it was clear they had not spent much time in this strange world.

I could imagine Tus and his tribe being friendly, as they had been to us, and then inviting them to a cookout. It was probably a joyful feeling, right up to when someone had cracked them in the head or punched a spear through them.

"I wonder how long the boat has been here. I wonder if the engine works."

I WONDER IF YOU'RE GOING TO ACTUALLY TRY AND START IT.

"Lock the door to the deck, Ned."

Ned sledded over to do just that. When I heard the door click, I said, "Hold your mouth just right," and then I turned the key.

Five

The motor made a choking sound, and when I thought it wouldn't catch, there was enough of a spark, and it cranked. It chugged and coughed, and then it roared, and finally motored down to a pleasant hum, like the buzzing of bees on a crowded hive.

There was a switch that had a piece of tape under it on which was written ANCHOR.

I flipped the switch. I heard a smaller motor whine. The anchor was being drawn up.

"Okay," I said, "here we go."

I WISH YOU HAD THE CAPTAIN'S HAT.

"I'm fine."

I WISH YOU HAD SOME PANTS.

"I'm fine."

The boat's paddle wheel began to churn, and the boat moved gently away from where it had been docked.

The wheelhouse had glass on three sides, and at the back was a smaller strip of glass you could use to look out on the back deck and beyond.

I glanced out of the glass to my right.

There was a huge cloud of smoke on shore. The tribe rushed to the edge of the lake. I have never seen so many disappointed faces. We had shit on their barbecue.

As the paddle wheel motored on, Ned wrote on his slate.

THEY ARE TAKING TO THEIR BOATS.

I glanced outside again. They certainly were, and now they were yelling a kind of war cry that might have served them well during the altercation with the rat-people. They must now be seriously hungry, and it had made them braver.

Ned was unhitching drawers and cabinets, all of which had small locks on them to keep from being jarred loose during rapid water or bad weather. He reached in and pulled out a gun. It was a six-shooter, old style. Or at least designed to look old style.

"I hope we will not need it," I said.

And I meant it. I would kill quickly and purposely if I felt a situation called for it, but I tried to avoid that kind of activity as a matter of course. It could become addictive.

Right then use of a pistol would have been handy. I was a little bit on the exhausted side after fighting off a horde of rat-people and being injured. I was at that moment physically no better than two or three men.

It was all moot. The steamboat chugged onward, and before long we had outdistanced them. Though hunger put them on the water and set them on pursuit, they gave up easily; fatigue perhaps. They knew they had lost the element of surprise, and they knew too, as I have said before, that I was no one to mess with. And Ned had the shock rod, and they had seen him use it. That little girl had really jumped and screamed. Another thing was we knew how to drive the boat, knew things they didn't know, and that is sometimes frightening enough. Knowledge certainly can be an effective weapon. Certainly, it was going to be a sad time at their barbecue. But they did say they had tubers. They roast up nice.

Per the gas gauge, we had a near-full tank. The boat would give us some protection and a chance to rest for a while, as we could spell one another at the controls. I was reasonably certain that though the river might wind about, it was ultimately heading toward the Blue Mountains. When I had been traveling through the trees earlier, I could see the river in the distance, in blue spots where there were gaps in the foliage, and those gaps were in the direction of the mountain range.

I thought of Jill, deep asleep and slowly dying, or maybe already dead.

I couldn't let that take my attention. It was counterproductive. To survive you had to take some items and place them on a shelf, to return to later, or to throw out later when its shelf-life was past due.

I was hoping Jill's shelf-life was a long one, but to worry consistently and without focusing on the duty at hand profited nothing.

I was determined to find the fleece and take it. After that, all I could do was hope Jill was still alive, and that the power of the fleece would do what jungle remedies had not.

I nudged the boat forward at a slightly faster pace, listened to the paddle wheels chop the water, and planned for success.

Ned had already fallen asleep, lying on his sled.

One

From the Journal of Bongo Bill

Suzie Q and I traveled through the trees and were fortunate enough to find fruit and birds eggs to supplement the small batch of edible goods we carried. We were a little too domesticated to enjoy the wild foods. The fruits were a little sour and made you shit frequently, and as for the birds eggs, we cracked them open and drank from the shells, and that was no treat either. Raw eggs are not high on my list of foods I want. Later, I would use my mess kit in my pack to fry them up, but at first we felt we were in too big a hurry, trying to keep up with Tango.

We did have the opportunity to groom one another, however, and that is the height of sophistication and a provider of small but juicy treats that reminded me of home during the better days, and it was nostalgically and culturally satisfying. The forests were rich in edible parasites.

Altogether, though, it wasn't much in the way of sustenance, but it kept us going.

We also found some trees with good wood for a bow, and we set about making one. I had in my supplies from Time Machine some thick cord, and that became the string for the bow. We used a knife to cut a nice limb and whittled it down so that it was reasonably balanced in thickness on both ends. I smoothed down the middle of it with my knife, and finally when we had what we thought might make a good bow, I applied the cord, pulled it from one end to the other by wrapping my leg around the bow so that I could hold it firmly and bend it.

The string was set. We then started looking for small limbs to be made into arrows. We didn't have metal arrowheads, or even stone, so Suzie Q and I used our knives to sharpen the ends of the arrows by whittling.

Suzie Q was still her excellent archer self; I did mention before how excellent a shot she was, and that's no exaggeration. She had it down. It wasn't a perfect bow and arrows, but over time Suzie Q managed to kill all of what she shot at, which was primarily birds. We gutted the creatures and cleaned them and cooked them on an open fire near an easy to access tree, in case a predator made an appearance.

Being a good cook, trained by my father, and having some condiments in my pack (couldn't help but bring them,) the birds, when we had them, were tasty. We had also, by this time, realized we were not going to keep up with Tango, so we took the time to pause to cook the eggs we found, and this was far more satisfying. A good egg should be cooked with a slick of oil or grease and then treated with dashes of salt and pepper, neither to be overdone. Hot sauce helps add to the flavor, but we didn't have that with us.

I can't say how long we had been traveling, but we had eaten and slept many times, as well as taken time to make the bow and arrows. As I mentioned, we were no longer trying to catch up with Tango.

From the tops of the trees we would set our course toward the mountain range, where on the other side, Tango said the people of the Golden Fleece lived.

It seemed so far away, but a lot closer than it had been before.

Progress.

It occurred to me more than once that except for the direction of the mountains, I had no idea where we were going. The other side of that vast range would go on for miles, and the chances of us finding the exact same place Tango was going to seemed limited.

So far, our adventure hadn't been all that adventurous, and I must say, Tango warned us. Still, the mountains seemed like some sort of plan, though a better plan might have been to return to Time Machine as Ned had done. The problem there was I was uncertain I could return to it. Our ancestors might have lived in the jungle and had sharp directional instincts, but I grew up quite differently than they did. I missed TV, my books, and the conveniences of a modern home and man-built plastic and metal trees to travel through the city when

I so chose to forgo four-wheeled transportation. Those "trees" had places to stop and drink from water fountains, and instead of having to make bows and arrows and hunt down birds, you could drop into one of the arboreal eateries and have a meal, and use the restroom, and not have to shit off a limb, or when on the ground, hunker up with my ass against a tree trunk and let it fly. There were also the parasite shops where we could, quite cheaply, I thought, purchase a bag of parasites or have them poured into our fur for personal or shared grooming. They were not as tasty as the parasites we found here in the jungle, but they were part of a ritual I missed; a trip to the parasite store.

I missed days that grew bright and then turned dark without benefit of cloud cover and high winds and storms. I missed days when it rained and I didn't have to be out in it, but could be in my home watching the rain run down a window glass in squiggly runnels.

Thinking of our old home and old way of life gave me pain because it only served to remind me of my parents, and the aliens, and the sinking ship, and the dreadful presidential asshole and his equally dreadful daughter Tomi. I was glad she and her father had drowned. I suppose I should have felt bad about that, but I did not.

It was during this period that I was feeling sorry for myself as we swung on limbs and vines through the trees, that Suzie Q whispered, "Stop. Wait."

I stopped, gave her a look.

She poked a finger downward.

Below in a clearing between thick swathes of trees was a small wild hog. It was noisily nosing up the dirt, trying to excavate roots and worms, whatever it was that wild hogs liked to eat, which I assumed might be just about anything.

The hog was long and plump, and whatever its choice of porcine, gourmet delights, it appeared from its physique that it was obviously successful at acquiring them. I had a sudden vision of sweet meat roasting over a slow fire. My mouth began to water.

Suzie Q eased an arrow from the crude quiver she had made of thick leaves and twine we had brought with us from Time Machine, and she nocked an arrow and aimed.

I will admit that though I was hungry, I was not overly hopeful that a sharpened stick would be enough to bring down a beast of that size. I fully expected the arrow to bounce off the beast's tough hide.

Suzie Q drew back the arrow and took aim and let the shaft fly. It hit the hog behind the left shoulder and went in deep. The hog leaped and twisted and then bolted for the deeper part of the jungle, but it hadn't gone far when its nose went down and it skidded on its belly and came to a stop.

I looked at Suzie Q. She looked as surprised as I felt. We climbed down cautiously and made our way to the hog. It was dead as our old life. We both laughed, then jumped up and down for joy. I took out my knife and tried to figure a way to skin the hog. I had about decided on a strategy when I heard a limb crack.

Suzie Q pulled an arrow from her quiver and put it to her bow with expert ease as they began to creep out of the forest.

Apes.

Two

There were many of them in the shadows of the trees, and remained so still that at first, I was uncertain what I was seeing. But once I realized they were there, and not a shadowy mirage, I began to see them better, as if all I had needed was the recognition of one to see them all. They were mostly on the ground, but some were in the trees, crouched on limbs. They didn't carry any weapons. They were more like us than traditional apes, our ancestors, but they didn't wear clothes.

They walked upright as they came out of the jungle. They carried a foul odor with them as they came. The last time they had bathed was when they had been caught in a rain. I was certain of that. They looked at us with curiosity, and they looked at the hog.

"Lower the bow," I said.

Suzie Q did just that.

The one in the lead, a large female, said, "We saw what you did, killing the hog. That is our hog."

"How do you figure?" Suzie Q said.

"You are two, we are many."

"That works for me," I said. "Enjoy."

I touched Suzie Q's shoulder, and we began easing back a bit toward the thicker jungle. The only problem here was I expected these beasts might follow. They were a heavier sort than us, but as they were recognizably close to our species, I assumed that though they might travel through the trees with greater caution, due to their weight, they could certainly make their way from limb to limb without undue effort.

"Wait," said the head ape, moving closer to us.

Now all the apes were in the clearing where we were, save for a few children and females who remained in the shadows of the trees.

"You speak our language," said the female.

"We speak all languages," I said.

"How can that be?"

"Magic," I said. It was science, of course, but considering my ability to understand it, it might as well have been magic.

My comment caused the lead ape to look back at her minions. Much hooting followed. These sounds, by the way, did not translate, but there was no doubt in my mind that they found the idea of magic intriguing.

"Why are you in our part of the jungle?"

"We apologize," I said. "We are lost. We are in search of friends. We were hungry. My sister killed the hog so that we might eat."

"We are hungry too," said the female.

"You are welcome to the hog," I said. "We merely want to leave in peace."

"Actually," Suzie Q said, "that is my hog, and I want to eat it. As much as I can eat of it, anyway."

The female ape snorted, and when she did, the other apes in the clearing came forward with their knuckles touching the ground. They had abandoned their upright state. They turned their heads from side to side. I know that trick, of course. I am an ape, or at least we were all of a similar make if not the same model. Their actions were a show of dominance, and it was best not to acknowledge it.

Still, that didn't keep Suzie Q from drawing her bow again.

"Lower the bow, Suzie Q."

She did, but reluctantly.

The female studied us for a long moment, then said, "Who do you seek?"

"A friend. Jack. Also known as Tango," I said. "But you would not know him."

The female ape snorted and made a noise in her throat that almost sounded like a chuckle.

"We know him. He is our friend too. He is family, even though he looks strange with no fur."

"True," I said.

"He is very strong and brave," said the female. "We fought together against the despicable rat-people."

"Rat-people?" Suzie Q said.

"The rat-people were many, and Tango was fighting bravely amongst people who looked more like him than us."

"Humans," I said.

"Yes. We failed to see his attraction to them. He didn't look as if he were about kill and eat any of them. He was protecting them."

"That sounds like Tango," I said. Or, I thought to myself, at least it sounds like the way he depicted himself, and the way Ned knew of him through novels and news reports. Tango the Monkey Man. How insulting a title. I could readily understand why he hated it.

"I am Rotah," said the female, "and by extension, you too are family. And you look more like us than him, so, shall we not all share in the feast? I will have the first cut of the meat, of course."

"Of course," I said. "Do you cook meat?"

The female studied me.

"That means using fire to make it sizzle," Suzie Q said.

"We have tasted such meat, in villages where we killed everyone and found meat in pots over fires. We have neither fire, or cooked meat. The fire hurt us. Jubog here, fire ate his toe. Show him, Jubog."

An ape of some size wandered out of the crowd and lifted his foot. Sure enough, he was missing a toe.

"I see that," I said. "We will be very careful. We will do the cooking, and we will all do the eating."

"Will you then show us how to make fire?" Rotah asked.

"We will certainly make that effort," I said. "So, shall we skin this meat and cook it? We can all share in the feast."

Rotah considered this, one hand to her chin, as if scratching a decision into existence.

The children and females that had remained behind in the jungle were inching forward now. I knew then it was all on the fence. They could take the meat, and us, and have a big meal, or they could allow us to cook the hog and share. I felt it could go either way.

"Yes. You are friends of Tango. Let's do it."

Three

It was quite a job, skinning and preparing that big hog by running a strong, sharp stick through its body, but we did that, and got it propped between forked supports harvested from the jungle, and pretty soon we had a fire going.

Hogs are frequently put in hot water and scraped of their hair, but skinning them is quite possible, and in the long run easier. I skinned and gutted it and put the guts aside on big leaves that Suzie Q gathered.

Not wishing to reveal our matches, for I had an inkling that Rotah would want those, I used the flint and steel kit I had, and along with dried leaves and small tinder, got the blaze going. I then asked for help, and Rotah sent out the apes to gather dry limbs, which they pulled up to the fire. I used them to keep the blaze burning. The flames licked up high, and the apes jumped back in astonishment.

Jubog of The Burnt Off Toe remained at a distance during the entire operation. When the fire was high and was licking at the meat, they all stood back in amazement, sniffing and hooting and bouncing about like kangaroos.

We got the hog lifted onto the forked sticks, and it was a delight to hear the meat crack and sizzle in the fire, and the smell was delightful.

I used my knife to carve off healthy pieces, and we all ate. When it came time for seconds, Suzie Q and I were out of the picture. The apes became excited and snatched at the meat. Now that the fire had burned down to coals they were much braver.

When the meal was over, the apes led us into the jungle until we came to another clearing where there was a clear pool of water. It wasn't a large pool, but we all squatted and cupped water up in our hands and drank from it. The water was clean and clear and sweet.

After our meal, they gathered some brush and ferns and made beds, and they made them for me and Suzie Q as well. I wasn't tired, or at least not enough to take a nap, but it seemed like the proper thing to do if we wanted to continue our quest at making friends. Probably not a good idea to ignore their customs, under the circumstances, and it was also a good way to collect parasites in our fur for later grooming. Suzie Q seemed perturbed about the whole thing and wanted to abandon the apes and take to the trees and go on toward the Blue Mountains.

I convinced her that our best course of action right now was not to disturb the rituals of the apes, as I felt we had to absorb their culture, at least temporarily, before we made our exit, or we might not make one at all. I had promised Rotah that I would teach her how to make and use fire, and I didn't want us to be their first personally cooked culinary experience. It was best that I be their chef for the time being. I knew from experience how much power that could wield and had considerable culinary skills of my own from all the time I had spent with my father in kitchens, watching him prepare meals, including those for the former President whose gourmet tastes ran to grease and sugar and air-filled slices of bread. If my father could stoop to conquer in the kitchen for someone like that, I could continue to roast hogs on spits, or make salads from fruits. A new career plan opened up for me. Chef to a tribe of unsophisticated apes, and if that seems like I'm putting myself on a pedestal there, I am not. But for the grace of location and education, Suzie Q and I could be in the same boat.

Their existence might have been simple, but their lack of interest or knowledge of fast cars and the latest fashions had freed them from unnecessary want. They lived their life freely and ate whatever they could find. Or whoever, I was quite certain.

It may not have been a noble existence, but their life mission was always clear. I supposed they didn't think to the future much, just to the present.

I, on the other hand, had future plans, and in my greedy and willful sophistication, I concocted one as I lay there on my bed of limbs and ferns, and it involved the ape band.

I felt a little guilty about it, but not so guilty I wasn't willing to have a crack at it. It seemed like the best thing I could come up with to secure mine and Suzie Q's safety. At least, as much safety as could be expected in a world like Down Under. I also should point out that I found Rotah quite attractive. She had the odor problem, but even that I had begun to find stimulating. It was musky and sexy in its own foul way. And her eyes, oh so dark and deep, and their custom of not wearing clothes didn't hurt my interest either. Still, it was just a thought, not a concern.

When I heard the others stirring from their naps, I sat up and asked if they might like me to prepare a small meal. We had eaten only a short time before, but living in the wild burned a lot of calories, so it was a good idea to eat when you could. Rotah was in quick agreement.

I asked for some assistance, and with Suzie Q in tow, as well as a couple of the apes, we went into the forest where I used my pack to contain several choice fruits and nuts from trees, and finally we turned over logs and scratched grubs up from the earth and put them in one of the plastic bags from our packs. When folded out, the bag was quite large, and within a short time, we had it packed with all manner of jungle treats, if you can call them that.

The Down World inhabitants knew how to find what I needed far more effortlessly than I did, and this, of course, made it an easier gathering that it would have been had it been left up to Suzie Q and me who were used to shopping in stores.

By the time we returned to the main camp, we had three bags full of roots and fruits, grubs and crickets, and I had stored all of this in my now-bulging pack. I began to dig a pit with my hands, and when the others figured out what I was doing, along with Suzie Q, they helped me dig. When I asked them to stop, we had a fairly good-sized hole. I stuffed it with kindling, started a fire using the flint and steel kit, added in heavier jungle wood, and soon had a substantial blaze.

Our distant cousin apes watched as I let the fire burn down. I then had Suzie Q pull the legs off the crickets, a dismal practice I assure you, but survival was our goal now. Suzie Q looked at me as if I had lost my mind, but she went about it, methodically, carefully opening the bags, grabbing crickets and pulling off their legs so they couldn't jump away.

I took my mess kit from my pack and, using some of the scraps of hog meat from the night before, rubbed the pan with it, greasing it up. I put the poor crickets in the pan a few at a time and cooked them legless and alive. I cooked a batch at a time in my small pan, and then poured the results onto large leaves and these became dinner plates for the apes.

I had them. They loved what I cooked, and for the next few days I convinced them to travel with us toward the Blue Mountains, constantly preparing meals in return for their protection.

Apes eat a lot, so it was demanding. These apes liked meat, roots, berries, whatever was available, but they especially liked it prepared by me. I was fully aware that at any interval in our journey they might turn on us and eat us, only missing my chef skills too late. But my plan was working in that we could move swiftly through the trees with them as our guardians, though they were anxious to stop often to eat or lie down where the sun was brightest through the gaps in the trees, and they enjoyed grooming marathons.

They didn't seem to have any real plans of their own, and they were happy to go where we went as long as they had cooked meals and naps.

So, it was ever onward, toward the ever closer, and in my view, foreboding, Blue Mountains.

One

Leo

Leo pulled at the harness and the leather bit into his hide. He tried to figure how long he had been pulling. Without the falling and rising of the sun, it was impossible to discern, but he tried nonetheless, as a means of taking his mind off the horror of the situation.

The harness had cut into his flesh and he had developed a wound across his right pec, and it was slow-bleeding constantly. What remained of his clothes had fallen into ruin. When they stopped, exhaustion put Leo straight to sleep, and then he was awakened either by yelling, lashes from a whip, or kicks in his ribs. It seemed as if he had only closed his eyes before he was back at it again.

As they went, slaves kept falling out, either too weak to continue, or dying on the spot. They were swiftly washed off and prepared for the evening meal. It was then, and only then, that the slaves were given extra rations, which included meat from slaves. The food was provided for those that the masters believed were the strongest. They wanted to keep the strong alive and let the weak die. Not really a sustainable policy, but that was the one used. Leo was one of the strong ones.

No talking was allowed between the slaves on threat of death, and even if it had been allowed, Leo couldn't understand the language, of even tell if they had the same language. It was all one grueling soul-sucking moment after another.

And then, suddenly they stopped, and Leo being in push position this day, looked up, and saw She Who Must Be Obeyed and Eats Lunch Early climb off her throne.

Leo didn't know what she was called, of course, but he knew she was the power and the horrible glory of this expedition, whatever its nature might be. From what Leo could tell it was about rolling over the earth, crushing and burning forests, using up wildlife as food, not to mention eating each other, and proceeding forward.

Was there a goal in mind beyond that? It was impossible to tell.

She came down and moved on large feet and elephantine legs, leaking pus and blood from boils and wounds from which little creatures exited and reentered. She had a stench that would have gagged a maggot and driven a skunk to suicide.

The beast of a woman, the it, walked like it wore concrete pants, throwing one leg way out, dragging the other behind it. One foot, the dragged one, was small and pink while the rest of the great beast was coated in a red fur that was falling out in patches, showing beneath it a white and leathery skin along with those wounds and boils.

Its head sat fat and bruised on a thick neck that was creased and banded like a concertina, and those crackling eyes were buried deep down in her fleshy head like raisins poked into a dirty snow bank. Her mouth draped open and things fell out of it. Some of the things that fell squirmed when they touched the earth.

The slaves cringed. Leo assumed he was about to see something he didn't want to see, and more fearful yet, he feared it might just involve him. He felt his soul rattle inside of him, like all that was him and all that were his ancestors were falling down stairs and cracking into pieces, like abused china.

It was a sensation that made him feel a fear he had never felt, and now he knew it was not just seeing this thing that did it, but he was feeling it as it came, raw sensations of pure evil, a steam roller of hate and flesh and electricity.

And then, belying its size and slow movement, suddenly it went into action. Its fat arms whipped out and the electricity in the fingertips sparked and sizzled and slaves were sent ass over heels. Blood painted the air, fell and dyed the ground. Splashes of it, hot and coppery smelling, slashed over Leo's chest as if someone had whipped a wet paintbrush through the air, snapping off red paint. This strange savagery went on for only a few seconds, and then she bent, and it was like watching someone trying to fold a giant parade float when she did that. She reached out, and pulled corpses to it. Her mouth gaped wide and the slaves' bodies were lifted and shoved into her gaping mouth head first, one at a time like appetizers. Lightning crackled in her mouth and rolled over her sugar cube-sized teeth with a sound like bees trying to fuck a lightning bolt.

Her mouth yawned wider, and the slaves' heads dissolved inside her expanding jaws, and she pushed the bodies deeper inside her mouth, and the meat turned to mush the color of bone and blood and flesh and shit, and still she pushed.

Leo stood still as a fencepost and watched her consume one dead body after another. It was sick and mesmerizing, like watching a python swallow a puppy.

Finishing with the dead, eating them, or perhaps dissolving them is more accurate, slowly she turned, and as she was about to waddle and drag her way back to the throne, she turned and glanced back at Leo.

It was at that moment the wind picked up and dark clouds blew in, racing across the sky. It was as if that damp, fleeting darkness inside of her were represented by those clouds. He felt something odd that wasn't entirely clear, but it came to him, and moved around inside his skull in emotional bursts. A young red-furred ape girl, constant rejection, abuse, a feeling of deep inferiority and a love for sweet things, and inside those emotions, like little spies, were strange alien impressions that jumbled and tumbled through her brain like insane, electric acrobats, and there was a feeling of something plastic and something metallic and all of it strange. A composition of power and inferiority, crackling electricity and dying dreams, a hatred that had little true design; that hatred rolled forward like the wheels on the great machine on which she rode. Hatred that was so powerful it preceded her. White-hot hatred that knew no bounds. It had color, and it had taste, and those images even had sound.

It was such a strong clutch of emotions that Leo felt as if his head was filling up, as if it were a bag stuffed too tight. She moved slightly toward him, and then the clouds, dark and damp, blew swiftly on, and the sun was bright, and he felt the emotions he had experienced move out of him like polluted water escaping a spillway.

Her eyes popped with fire and there was a wisp of smoke that rolled out of the corners of her mouth and out of her nostrils; and then she turned. A switch had been flipped. She was about another chore, climbing back up on her throne.

Leo knew he had been spared by nothing other than a moody whim. His strength nearly deserted him, and for a moment he felt drained of all that made him human, felt as if he would collapse right there to be whipped and cursed, and he knew too that if he collapsed, he might not rise, and the wheels would roll and he would be tenderized, served up later as part of a meal.

For a moment, a fleeting moment, he didn't care. But then his strength returned (what little was left of it) and he stood firm. He dug way down deep inside and looked for hope. It was in a shadowed corner, but he got it by the ear, so to speak, and yanked it into duty.

I must live.

I must go on.

Up she climbed, laboriously, uncanny strength wrapped in a damaged hulk. Her eyes sparkled. Her ass farted a puff of fire. She found her position on the throne and settled in.

A whip cracked. Leo felt it on his back. Yells came. Groans came.

He began to push again. Onward, toward the Blue Mountains.

Two

They advanced, over a swath of trees with the great machine in the fore, the smaller machines spread out on either side, over the jungle the machines went, smashing it down.

Snakes squirmed in all directions. Big ones, little ones, colorful ones, dull ones. There were huge balloon-like blooms in tall, falling trees, and they were loosened by the machines, set free on the wind; they floated like party balloons; most were silver, some were blue, a few yellow, colorful, but transparent.

The machines rolled on, trees and earth cracking beneath them, flattened into mulch.

Squish and crunch.

Roll on.

Roll on.

One

From the Journal of Bongo Bill

We moved through the trees and sometimes across the ground, and me and Suzie Q scrounged, and I cooked, and she practiced with her bow to the amazement of the apes.

Suzie Q would have an ape toss a piece of fruit high and she would shoot an arrow right through it. Damn, she should have had her Olympic shot. She had an eagle eye and was steady as a statue, never a tremble or a breath too sharp. She loosed arrows with a beautiful delicacy, sent them into their targets smooth and clean.

She rarely missed, and never by wide margins.

I remember one day we were moving through the trees, and I could see great plant balloons floating in the sky, masses of them, all manner of colors. I had become accustomed to them as of late. There were parts of the jungle where they grew in multitudes, and we had been traveling through a section like that for some time. I assumed they came loose when they were ripe and ready to spread their seeds, which were contained inside of them; small and light and misty. I had seen a few of them snag on limbs, explode and scatter the seeds. Either that, or something had knocked them loose of their moorings. Before, I had only seen a few at the time, but the sky, close and distant, was full of them.

It was then that the jungle thinned, and we were at the base of a rocky trail that led up into the mountains. Off to the left I saw a great river, and on its other side, tall trees. Above that, the plant balloons filling the sky.

Now, where to go?

Then I heard a puffing sound and saw smoke rising up. It was coming from the river.

It was a steamboat paddling its way along, and on the deck, sunning, belly up, was Ned the Seal.

Two

Me and Suzie Q moved swiftly through the trees and tried to get ahead of the steamboat. We barely managed that. The river narrowed where we stopped, and there was a huge, leafy tree limb that spread out over the edge of the water, making a shadow thick as an oil spill. We watched the boat come. Rotah and the other apes followed after. Only Rotah came out on the limb to sit beside us. She sat beside me, actually. I didn't mind that.

The other apes were on the shore, half-hidden in the jungle, watching.

We sat on the limb and waited as the boat came paddling along, puffing little white smoke that smelled like the steam from boiling water.

I saw Tango then, through the front glass of the wheelhouse. I could tell he saw us. The boat slowed and the puffing stopped. Tango came out to the bow of the boat, and following him on his sled, Ned came, pushing his fez onto his head.

"That is him," said Rotah. "The big white man who acts and sounds and fights like an ape and has a really big dick."

I thought maybe Tango could use a new loin cloth, or a pair of pants. That thing was distracting.

As the boat neared, I grabbed Suzie Q's hand, and lowered her down so that she could drop onto the deck of the paddlewheel. She hugged Tango, then leaped at Ned and hugged him.

Rotah took my hand and lowered me down, and then she swung to the deck and landed gracefully, but with a loud kerthump.

"My cousin, Rotah," Tango said.

Rotah slapped her chest. "Cousin Tango. Greetings."

"One moment," Tango said, eased back into the wheelhouse. I heard a motor and a splash. Realized the anchor had been dropped. We drifted on the water.

The apes had moved out of the jungle now and were on the shoreline, observing.

"You have managed a sweet ride," I said.

"We have," Tango said.

Ned wrote on his slate.

IT PUFFS WHITE SMOKE AND RUNS ON GAS BUT CAN RUN ON WOOD. IT'S PRETTY COOL.

"It is cool," Suzie Q said.

"We were looking for you, trying to reach the mountains. Rotah here has been very helpful. I have been cooking for her and her tribe."

"I see," Tango said. "Then, we shall proceed there. What of you, Rotah? Are you going with us to the mountains? There may be a fight, and it's not your fight."

"Rotah likes a good fight. And something to eat. Haven't had a good hump in a while, though."

Rotah looked at me.

I felt embarrassed, to say the least.

I looked at Tango. He shrugged.

Ned wrote: ONWARD THEN.

"What of your tribe?" I asked Rotah.

She went to the edge of the boat and yelled out: "I go to fight in the mountains. You can fight or stay. But if you come, you must go by the trees and follow the river."

There was a wild moment of hopping and chest-beating from the apes on shore, and when that display was completed, they immediately took to the trees and started moving through them where they grew along the edge of the river.

"Good," Tango said. "We appreciate your help."

"We are cousins," Rotah said.

"That we are. That we are."

Tango returned to the wheelhouse. We heard the anchor go up. We heard the main engine cough to life, and once again the paddle boat started moving along the riverway.

Ned wrote on his slate.

TANGO REALLY NEEDS SOME PANTS.

Three

There was fishing equipment on board, and we fished daily, and that was our main food. There was cooking oil and flour and other kinds of cooking items stocked in the shelves and drawers, and I did the cooking. I was really tired of fish by the time the river began to wind through the Blue Mountains, along a narrow stretch with great rises of stone on either side.

I would like to point out that Ned never tired of fish. Every time we awoke from a sleep, and it was something we took turns at, with either Tango at the wheel, or Ned, on a stool, steering with his thumb-enhanced flippers, Ned would produce his slate and write: WHEN ARE WE HAVING THE BREAKFAST FISH?

Later it would be: IS IT LUNCH FISH YET?

A FISH SNACK WOULD BE BRACING.

IS IT DINNER FISH YET?

YOU KNOW WHAT WOULD BE NICE? A BED SNACK OF FRIED FISH, OR RAW, OR BOILED.

The little guy could hardly think of anything else.

Sometimes, we would be cruising along, and I would see Ned's eyes wet, as if tearful, and he would take his slate and write.

I REALLY LIKE FISH. I APPRECIATE THE WAY YOU PREPARE THEM. I CAN EAT THEM RAW, THOUGH. YOU ARE A GOOD MAN.

It was a roomy boat, and riding on it was one of the more pleasant aspects of our adventure so far. We went along for many sleeps through the split in the mountains, and over some rapid waters that I thought we might fail to negotiate, but Tango managed them skillfully. He told me he had lived a long time, even long enough to have been a river pilot.

He told me an interesting story about him and a lycanthrope on the steamboat he piloted, which was called THE WESTERN STAR, which was named after the WESTERN STAR STAGE LINE, the company that owned the boat, as well as a number of banks and a handful of brothels.

The story was exciting, a kind of who's the werewolf on board adventure that took place as they made their way down the river. I wasn't sure I believed such a story. It sounded preposterous to me, though Tango didn't seem like the lying type. I suspect having lived on a world with a president who would rather tell a lie than the truth had damaged my acceptance of any truth. Old Dunderhead had told so many lies he couldn't keep up with them, and neither could anyone else. He told them until they were the norm. If you are bathed in lies enough, nothing seems true; you are always wet and never dry.

One good thing, though, as we went, Tango taught me how to manage the boat. I like to believe that I became quite skillful, if far from expert.

Eventually the river opened wide, and we chugged out onto a great lake surrounded by mountains, and that's when we pulled the boat close to shore and anchored it.

"From what I understand, the place I seek, the home of the Golden Fleece, is on the far side of that mountain. The bluest of the Blue Mountains, I was told."

And blue the mountain was, low down and way high. It was made of a kind of stone that looked a lot like slate, but it was dark blue and the central sun made the stone shine and seem bluer yet. The other mountains around were bluish as well, but there was a patchwork of color in their stones, red and blue and yellow, and dark stones that seemed the very essence of night. They did not rise as high as this mountain, but any one of them seemed a formidable challenge. But then Tango said something that, at least to me, seemed hopeful.

"I was told that not too far up, there is a path in the mountains, and that it leads through a split in the mountain, and on the other side is the place we seek. If that is correct, we are not that far away, and we wouldn't actually have to go over the top, just through the passage."

That was good news.

And what of the apes?

They had not arrived yet, but Rotah assured us that they would come, and that she herself would go out and find them if need be. We had probably motored far ahead of them, but they would arrive, she said, because she had told them to and they had indicated they would.

No contracts were signed. No threats had been made. Rotah had said, and they would do.

That was her view, anyway. I wasn't sure. The apes seemed like a lazy bunch to me. I assumed they had stopped somewhere along the way to eat fruit and had forgotten all about the mission, and Rotah.

I had, in a short time, become a cynical bastard.

Four

I hated to leave the comfort of the boat, and of course there was no guarantee it would be there when we came back, but there was nothing else for it.

We packed up a number of things, and then with Tango leading, Ned on his sled, and me and Suzie Q following, we set out. Rotah had gone back to catch up with her tribe and guide them to us, now that she knew where the split in the mountain was generally supposed to be.

I admit to feeling sad when she left, and especially because she had leaned over and kissed me on the head. I was amazed and a little delighted. I hoped to see her and her tribe again, especially her, but a part of me, the part that had grown cold and cynical, thought that once she was gone, out of sight, out of mind.

It was a tough trek, and much climbing was involved. I hoped ceaselessly that the next moment would reveal the pass through the mountains, but up we went. Up and up.

Tango never seemed to tire, and Ned negotiated better than all of us, having the sled to help him climb, but as it leaned in more precarious places, I feared he would slide out of it, but he was able to maintain quite well; the sled was almost like a part of him.

Suzie Q and I brought up the tail end, and from time to time we had to rest and try and catch up later. We always caught up, but sometimes Tango and Ned were a considerable distance ahead of us, and I think they slowed down to make it easier for us.

At a time when I felt I couldn't possibly go on, we rounded a sharp rocky curve at a precarious place where the mountain dropped off into a stony crevasse, and the path became wider and smoother.

Tango and Ned were waiting on us. Tango was smiling and Ned was sort of vibrating in a manner that made it look as if he were trying to jump. All he managed was a rising and settling of his body on his sled.

We hustled over to them and looked out to where Tango was pointing. The rocky crevasse didn't extend to where we now stood. Just below us was jungle, and where it ended was a gently sloping green valley, and on the far side of it, nestled near another mountain range, was an incredibly large city with shiny white stone plazas. Pyramids rose up high, and were painted all manner of colors, and there were a variety of smaller structures, including what I deduced to be homes. They were large and reminded me of beehives, or hornet nests, and they were made of stone as well, but in this case, the blue stone that was the distinguishing feature of the mountain. Streets of white stone were laid out between the rows of beehive homes, and all of them led eventually led to the largest and central pyramid. The colors on that pyramid were the brightest, and they depicted snakes and birds. Around the city, stretching for miles, was a tremendous wall etched with designs and colorful paintings, but from our perch we could see over it and into the city.

Beyond the city, just before the back-mountain range rose, was a whirling mass that came down from above. It was impossible to tell exactly what was in the mass. It was broad and sometimes bright and sometimes dark, and it was constant. We watched it for a long time but could never draw any satisfying conclusions.

"I was told the fleece was kept in a large pyramid, and that must be it," Tango said. "But this is amazing. Even I who have seen much, have not seen anything like this. And the cyclone at the back of the city, it never moves from its spot."

"Now we have to go down there and convince them to give you the fleece," I said.

Ned honked his horn in agreement.

Five

There was a thin trail at first, but then it became a wide one that led through the large patch of jungle and into the valley and city below. Without realizing it, we had found the split in the mountains. We had been on our needed path before we knew we were on it, though I wouldn't have been surprised if Tango had suspected.

It was still a long way down, longer than it looked from our high roost, and we stopped and camped a number of times as we proceeded toward the city. There seemed to be an endless number of the trees with the balloon-like plants on them, and the birds and animals were thick.

We saw several herds of dinosaurs but were able to avoid becoming their lunch. They thundered though broad paths in the jungle that most likely they had made over time.

It was amazing how common all the wonders of this world now seemed, including dinosaurs.

Finally, we were at the base of the valley, and we came to a wide road of yellow bricks that led to the city. We could see the great wall from where we were, and the tops of the large pyramids inside the city. The designs on the wall and the pyramids seemed less bright from this position, but no less impressive, especially the largest pyramid which rose much higher than the others.

As we came closer, we could see the giant wooden gates were thrown open. We didn't hesitate. We were on a mission. We made our way through the open gateway. No one tried to stop us. No one did anything, because there wasn't anyone around.

I heard a bit of scuttling here and there, and I told Suzie Q to be ready to nock her bow. Tango had a knife he had brought from the steamboat, and it was a big thing with a bone hilt and a wide hand

guard. He had made himself a sheath for it, and had kindly consented to wear a loin cloth made from a blue towel. It threaded through the belt for the knife and had a long flap in front and back.

Deeper into the city we went, and we could see grass growing up through cracks in the stone. Though beautiful, on closer inspection, it looked like a place that had worn out its own welcome.

And then we saw people stick their heads out of the open doors of the cone-shaped houses and out of the square-cut windows, and finally there were people in the street. Their numbers were few, and they were a ragged bunch. They walked toward us with caution, as if trying to traverse hot coals with their bare feet.

Eventually, a man who wore a colorful vest and trim blue pants and looked as if he had once been noble but was now working hard to hold his head up, came toward us. He had his arms spread in an I Am Not an Enemy position. He had a smile on his face, but it was a thin one.

"Warriors," said the man in the colorful vest and trim pants, "there is no need for violence. We are peaceful, and will share with you what we have, though it is not much."

"You need have no fear," Tango said. "We are peaceful as well. Unless someone here gets nasty, then we will be less peaceful."

Ned honked his horn in agreement.

"What is that?" said the leader, gesturing to Ned. "Is it real?"

Ned's mouth fell open. He wrote on his pad.

ARE YOU KIDDING.

"What's that say?" said the vested man.

I had forgotten the injection had given us the ability to understand language, but not writing of different forms.

Ned wrote again. I'M REAL AND I AM A SEAL.

"He says he's a seal," Suzie Q said.

"A what?" asked the man.

"It would take some explanation," Tango said. "Listen, it may be bad manners to bring this up immediately, but it seems the city has been through something."

"Oh, it has at that," said the man in the colorful vest and trim pants. "If you come in peace, we welcome you. If you come in war, we have nothing to give you and nothing to fight with."

"You have larger numbers," Tango said.

The man nodded, but the subject of numbers didn't interest him. "What has happened to us is not due to invaders, but due to within. Shall we eat and drink?"

It was nice talk, but I was still being cautious. It seemed too simple and easy.

They led us to the great pyramid. There was a wooden door at the opening. They opened it, and we cautiously went inside. Everything seemed like a trap to me after being in this inner world for whatever time we had been here, so I remained on high alert. If Tango was concerned, he didn't show it, and that was something of a relief. Something about Tango generated confidence and inner wisdom.

The interior of the pyramid was lit with torches, and there were some scrawny-looking men sitting on stone benches around the wall. They looked as if they had just finished a day at a foundry.

The torches gave the inner room light, but it was a weak, flickering, buttery light. There was a great stone dais in the center of the room, and there were some wicker seats pulled up to it, and that's where we were asked to sit, along with our main host and several of his people. The rest found positions on the stone benches around the room or seated themselves on the floor.

Ned cruised his sled to the dais, held up his slate so Tango could see it, but I could see it as well.

I FEAR CANNIBALISM

Tango smiled, said, "Be calm."

"We know you must be wary of us," said the man in the vest, "but we mean you no harm. My name is Goseff. Once we were a great city, and people came from miles around to trade with us, to live here, but in time we feared those with different customs, that looked different, like your apes here, and we built the great wall around the city. In time, we grew stagnant. No new flesh. And our customs grew stale. Trade dried up. We had decided to protect ourselves completely, cut ourselves off from the pollution of anything new and different. It didn't work out. We had plenty then, and we had a beautiful city. We worked constantly to make the coating that covers the stones in the plaza; it was our greatest industry, the city itself.

"To make the coatings for the stones, all except the blue stones, we had to burn the stone to break it down and make the slick white coating you see in the city. There were many trees then. Trees in the city that offered shade, and there were trees immediately outside the city that were full of fruit and provided other animals for hunting. But when the trees were cut to make the firewood that melted the stone to make the coating we so loved, we eliminated much of our food source. Many trees remain, but there were so many in the city at that time, that the loss of so many trees, the covering of farmland with stone to make our city great, made our city less great, and people began to migrate away. We leave the gate open now, hoping they will come back. But to what? An empty city that has no farmland. The trees have grown back in many places, and the jungle is near again, but the damage was done. We had more city than we had food. A stigma rests on this city as surely as a cloud."

"There is food," Tango said. "It would require work, but there is food. The jungle is close enough and there is plenty to eat if managed properly. And, as you said, you could pull up and break up stone and make gardens and farms."

"Our spirit is broken, and I don't see us having it back."

This seemed outside the realm of what Tango, the ever resourceful, could understand, but he merely made a grunting noise and accepted Goseff's evaluation.

Food was brought then. I don't know who signaled who to get that done, but the food came and was placed on the dais, and we ate.

It was a simple meal made of stringy meat of some sort, with fruit and vegetables. It was hardly a meal to match the great pyramid. I could see there three pathways that led from the chamber and disappeared into darkness. I wanted to feel comfortable and secure, but those flickering torches, and those dark passageways, the oddity of our host and his people made me feel as if at any moment they might spring.

From the looks of them, they might not actually be able to spring, but maybe they could stumble a little.

When we finished our simple meal, which was more like an appetizer for a child, our host smiled and looked at us so sadly I almost wanted to comfort him.

"Why have you come?" said our host. "What do you seek?"

"Since you are direct, I will be straight with you," Tango said. "My wife is ill. She may not recover, but I've been told there is a fleece, a golden fleece, the Golden Fleece, and that not only is it the source of legends and mythologies, but that it actually cures. I would like to make a bold suggestion that you loan it to me, go with me as I use it, so that you can be assured of its return, whatever deal you might like to strike I am willing to entertain. I love her. She is in a bad way, and if the fleece will cure her, I would like its use. I have no desire to retain it."

"Ah. The fleece," said our host. "Well, before we go farther, I should have your names. You have mine."

We gave our names. Ned wrote his name on his slate out of habit, and Tango said it aloud to Goseff.

"I want you to know that I, Goseff, speak to you as a friend. The fleece, it exists, but it has never cured anyone of anything."

"That is not what we've heard," Tango said.

Goseff nodded. "I know. But it is true nonetheless. Once we had great men and women of medicine, and they cured many things. But the power of the fleece was merely a legend. We let it be a legend. It gave our city an air of mystery, and before we built the wall, people came from miles around to see it at the yearly presentation. I would bring it out and take it to the peak of this structure, and hold it up so that the light of the sun made it glow. Outsiders and insiders would bring the sick, and several would be chosen, and the fleece would be put around them, but it never actually cured anyone of anything. It was a suggestion of cure, nothing more. Our medicine people did cure many, but they are long gone now, along with all the secrets they possessed. As for the fleece, I was one of his priests. A false job. But it was my job, and now I am a kind of leader for these people. We have thrown away pretense. We have had to."

Goseff stood and walked over to the far wall. There was an indentation in the wall. He reached in and pulled out a folded cloth. He brought it to the dais, pushed the plates aside and placed it in the center. He unfolded it. It was a fleece and it was gold. But it was ratty and much of the wool had fallen out, so there was almost as much raw-looking skin visible as fleece itself. The gold was faded to the color of old mustard.

"We no longer upkeep it. No one comes to see us. The legend is out there, but we are hard to find, which I suppose under our current circumstances is good. We can't defend ourselves. We have weapons, but no one who uses them, nor do we want to use them. We are a people of peace. I am sorry. The fleece is a lie."

Tango stood up, reached out and took hold of the fleece. All the confidence that was in him drained. His broad shoulders slumped and his knees bent as he picked up the fleece and sat down again, looking at it like a diseased pet.

"We used to sprinkle it with gold dust, when we had gold, and the gold would make it bright in the sun. But cure? It never cured anything. My position, the position of all the priests, was one of privilege. We got the best of everything offered, because we were the protectors of the fleece. Only it was just the skin of some poor creature who had the misfortune to possess what was once a beautiful pelt. It held no secret healing properties. It is as you hold it; even less than what it was, and strictly speaking, that was nothing. It was an empty promise and people believed in it not because it did anything, but because they wanted to believe. Faith. But faith is not enough. Faith in promises too big and magical to be true is faith in nothing."

"I am disappointed," was all Tango said.

Ned wrote: SORRY

Tango reached out and patted Ned on the back of the head, causing the tassel on his fez to swing.

"It is only what it is," Goseff said.

It was like the air went out of the room. We knew then what Tango obviously knew. There was nothing he could do for Jill.

"I am truly sorry for your loved one, and I wish there was something I could do for you," Goseff said. "We are nothing more than this sad bunch, perhaps there are two thousand souls sprinkled about the city. Once there were so many of us we bumped against one another in the streets. No longer. Our city is doomed, as are we. Even now our doom approaches. We have heard from travelers like yourself that a great army approaches us. Travelers is a kind word. They were fleeing before the army, and some of those who came here were escaped slaves. They had scarred backs and festering wounds from their captivity. This army, they say it tears everything down in its path, and we are in their line of march."

"Perhaps the wall isn't such a bad idea in that case," Suzie Q said.

"Two sides to everything," Goseff said. "I understand that. But they are not coming here to trade, or to live with us, they are coming here to conquer us, and if what we have heard is correct, they will destroy us and all that is here, and move on again. They are like a living plague."

Ned beeped his horn, wrote on his slate.

I HAVE SEEN THEM. THERE ARE A LOT OF THOSE ASSHOLES. THEY ARE CRUSHING EVERYTHING IN THEIR PATH. THEY HAVE SLAVES.

Tango translated the words on the slate as our host could not read it.

"Ah, I suppose we made our path, and the irony is that now that we have fallen into ruin, what we feared then when we were mighty, is certain now. We are condemned by fate, and we deserve it."

"You talk defeat before the need," Tango said. "You have time to leave. You have at least that."

"To where? We know nothing but this. We don't know how to survive any other way, and this isn't exactly an endearing way of life."

WHAT THEY HAVE PLANNED WILL NOT BE A NAP AND A QUICK BLOW FROM A HAMMER.

Ned had written that quickly, and now Tango translated.

"But what are we to do?"

"One thing," Tango said, tossing the fleece onto the dais, "is learning to move on when things go bad. Learning to continue."

"We understand the idea," Goseff said, "but not the purpose."

"Meaning you would rather whine about your lot in life than do something."

Goseff looked at him. "You are strong and magnificent, and you believe in something. There is nothing left for us to believe."

"Any idea how long it will take the attackers to arrive here?"

"A few weeks, I suppose."

"Perhaps there is a way," Tango said. "Ned here saw them up close. We talked about it on our journey down the great river. The army is led by one powerful being. A strange creature, according to Ned."

WICKED UGLY. FARTS THUNDER AND FIRE. STARES AT YOU WITH ELECTRICITY.

Tango didn't translate that exactly. He said, "This leader, who may be female, is bad news."

"That's the only news we have these days," said Goseff. "All I can offer you is this worthless fleece for your efforts, and my best wishes."

One

From the Journal of Ned the Seal

I have written all of this using the stories told by all of us, and all of our versions of what happened.

Bill is a talker. He tells you everything. I do not. I tell you what I think is worth telling. So, I am going to put a lot of this in a nutshell so we can get to the good part.

Ready?

Of course you are.

But one thing I want to note here. The great city had no fish. No one had fish. It was nuts and berries and roots and some kind of cooked something or another that might have been rat, and not fat rat at that. Whatever it was, I ate it. I ate whatever. I'm a unique seal. But, no fish. So, if you ever visit there, be sure and bring lots of dried fish, Norwegian style.

Just a note.

They gave the fleece to Tango to assure him that it wasn't a thing they were concerned with anymore. Tango took it, tied it around his neck with the skin of the front legs, and wore it.

We were given an empty cone house to stay in, and we took turns sleeping, not entirely trusting our host and his followers. But, we all felt that they had about as much energy as a corpse, so I can't say we were overly worried. Our plan now was simple. Return to the village where Jill was dying or dead. Tango thought there might be a chance she would be alive and he could be at her side. If she was dead, he wanted to be there to mourn her.

As always, Tango was practical. He wanted us to rest and eat as well as was possible before we started back. It was his idea we could make nearly all the journey by steamboat.

While we rested, I wrote out all I had seen, and Tango read it aloud so I didn't have to hold up the slate while each one of them read at their own pace. I could write and Tango could put it out there quickly to be absorbed.

I filled everyone in on what I had seen before I met up with Tango. I had told Tango this, of course, but Bill and Suzie Q didn't know about it. I told them about the tar from the pits, the great machines powered by slaves, the vast army, and then I told them something that I had not thought to tell Tango, as I was unaware of its personal significance to him. I told Tango I had seen a black man among them, and when I described him, Tango said—

"Leo. He lives."

Then we all got a lesson from Tango about who Leo was. A friend. A companion, and a jack of all trades. But, he was now a slave.

When Tango finished telling us about Leo, I continued my story, told them about the big woman who farted fire and coughed lightning.

Finished with my story, Tango leaned back in the simple wicker chair he was sitting in and stared at the ceiling for a time. None of us spoke.

Eventually, Tango said, "I know what I must do, but what I do is not necessary for any of you to do. I respect your choices. But me, I cannot bring the fleece to Jill, as it is worthless, except to wear around my neck, and though I want to go home and be with her until the end, her death is inevitable. Leo's is not. I intend to rescue him. I will try and stop the army."

I wrote: YOU WILL BE VERY BUSY

Tango laughed. "I can imagine. But where there is a will there is a way. That's what they lack here. A will. I have enough will for many people. No brag, merely a fact."

None of us were questioning his will, but his judgment seemed suspect.

"How far away would you say this army is?" Tango asked.

I AM NOT SURE. I WOULD SAY FAR, BUT NOT THAT FAR. TOPSIDE IT WOULD TAKE SEVERAL DAYS. WEEKS. TIME IS HARD HERE.

"Let me think on it," Tango said, and tying the fleece around his neck, he rose and left the cone house.

Two

Tango came up with a plan all right, but the rest of us added bits and pieces. It was made up of several ideas, but the first piece of the plan was we made a great web constructed of vines and ropes that the city dwellers gave us.

We made a web so large it could hold several hundred of the gassy plants that grew in the trees outside of the city. When we filled the net with them, the net rose, and it was held to the ground by only a rope. We had built a wheelhouse of sorts under the web, and there were a number of bags of stones for ballast. There was an opening at the top of the wheelhouse through which we could exit, and there was one at the bottom; both openings were covered by trap doors. It was actually kind of snazzy. Of course, we had yet to figure out how to steer it, but Tango saw that as a minor problem. I saw it as a mite larger than that.

The jungle was searched for snakes and poisonous spiders. There were a lot of them. It was not fun catching them, and after the first day, I pretended to come down with something and stayed in the cone house. I don't like snakes or spiders. I do not like eels either. I merely thought I would mention that.

Tango and the ape folk brought the creatures back in bags and the bags were loaded into the wheelhouse. The people in the city found what we were doing curious, but mostly they stood around the great gassy plant-filled bag and stared at it.

In the meantime, Tango finally convinced the city folk to help by weaving another net and asking them to stuff it with the gassy plants, done to his specifications.

The city folk had pretty much accepted their fate until he convinced them to do that, and then suddenly they were inspired. Tango was like that. He was inspiring. I can be very inspiring until I get tired.

Now they were energized, and when they saw Suzie Q practicing with her bow and arrow, Goseff led us to a small pyramid and took us inside. The place was stuffed with weapons. Spears, bows and arrows, clubs made of shiny black wood, and there were sharp stones embedded in the wood. They were nasty devices.

I didn't take anything, as I had my stun rod. My flippers, even with thumbs, are not that greatest for tossing spears or shooting arrows. I have learned how to do such things with a whipping of my body, but in the end, the game isn't worth it. What I could use best was the stun rod and could also flee rapidly on my sled. I expected a lot of fleeing.

There was also armor and round shields made of wood and leather, and I did choose a leather helmet and a breast plate that I felt I could rework to cover my body to some extent.

The city folks then began to want lessons in the bow and arrow from Suzie Q, and she gave them. She was an amazing shot. The spirit to fight had been awakened in most of them, and pretty soon we had a bit of an army going, if you can call a bunch of formerly morose farmers who sat on their asses all the time and pissed and moaned about how things had gone to hell, an army.

Still, it beat going into battle with just the four of us.

Once, during a rest time, in our cone house, Tango said, "You know we have about as much chance as a snowball in hell? An army of four has its limitations."

"We have much more than that now," Bill said.

"They are playing soldier," Tango said. "First time the attackers yell, they'll run."

I wasn't sure if Tango meant that, or if he was just down in the dumps, but it was the most negative thing I had ever heard Tango say. After that, he became more silent than usual, and spent a lot of time at the edge of the city looking off into the jungle.

We all eventually decided to head toward where the great swirling went on, the debris that was falling from the sky. It was a long trek, but we felt it was worth it, because it struck us that there might be something there we could use. It also seemed to reinvigorate Tango a little, and I was anxious for him to be his old self. I liked it when he inspired me, not when I was attempting to inspire him.

The stronger of the city folk, now wearing armor and armed, came with us. They had vowed to fight. They had been inspired by our industry. They had also suggested the trip. They said that many of the tools and weapons they had in their storage room had been made from objects found at that site.

The armor fit them loosely and they carried their weapons poorly. Of course, my helmet of leather fit me poorly as well, and I found the breast plate more trouble than it was worth. It wasn't like I was going to stand up and walk, so my back was exposed. Eventually, with Tango's help, I turned it into lighter armor that covered both my back and stomach area. It was mostly wishful thinking that it would protect me from anything seriously launched, but sometimes a bit of wishful thinking doesn't hurt, though too much of it leads to nothing more than wishful thinking.

When we came to the swirling, we could see way up and it was dark up there at the top, and the debris kept coming. It was fragments of this and that, but on the ground where the stuff piled up, there were the remains of airplanes and boats and automobiles that were a time well ahead of the time in which I was born. I recognized a lot of it, though. Remember, me and Wells had been time and dimensional travelers.

"Somehow these things have crossed from other times and worlds to find their way here," Tango said.

"How?" Suzie Q asked.

"There are holes in time."

I honked my horn in agreement. Been there, done that.

"So, the sky done ripped," Suzie Q said.

"Not just the sky, little one. The very fabric of time and space. These things have come from many worlds. It's a time and space portal. That's the extent of my knowledge."

I WISH WELLS WAS HERE, I wrote.

Tango nodded. "He might shed more light on it."

The debris on the ground was varied. Some looked new, a lot looked old and was rusted and rotting. Goseff, who was with us, said that once there had been a great chasm here, but the things had fallen for so much time that the chasm had been filled in. He said he remembered when the falling began. He was a boy then. The sky had ripped open and things began to come out of it. Sometimes humans, dead when they hit the debris, of course. Maybe dead before. The city folks had ground them up and used them for fertilizer back when they were a prosperous city. Now, if bodies came through, human or animal, the great birds and the insects, the animal scroungers ate them. They didn't lie about long. But the other things were merely covered by other fallen objects, pushed down by the added weight, though as of late, the former chasm was starting to overflow.

"Seems eventually it will spread, because where else can it go," Bill said. "The impact of new items will cause things to be blown out wider. In time, it could fill all of Down World. It would be some time, as a lot of it rots or rusts away, but it could happen. I think the city should have a plan for removal and disposal."

"I believe you are right," Tango said. "But look there. Do you see that airplane, the one with double wings? That is a Fokker, and it appears intact."

As we stood there, more items smacked the pile, and it was only by mere accident that the Fokker had been pushed to the side, and left, for the most part, undamaged, though one of its top wings was shattered.

"I can fly that plane if it's serviceable," Tango said. "If only Leo were here. He was handy with mechanical things."

I wrote, I AM PRETTY DAMN HANDY.

"Of course," Bill said. "Ned worked with Wells on the time traveling machine. He knows a lot."

THAT'S RIGHT.

"Very well then. Let's bring the ropes and fasten them to the things we need and remove them, without being crushed by the falling wreckage, of course. We should start with the Fokker."

This seemed a wise choice, as it had mostly been pushed out of range of the continuously tumbling objects.

The city folk were a bit confused by what we were asking them to do, but eventually they figured out the gist of it, and we fastened ropes and tugged the plane well out of the way of the whirling mass of this and that.

Then we went after other items.

Some of those were more precarious to claim, but Tango was brave about stepping into the midst of it all, a rope around his waist, debris crashing all around him, and the sky storm pushing down on him, but he managed to hook some things he wanted up with the ropes, and with the aid of our new army, we were able to pull them out.

It was a tedious day, and Tango once got hit by what he said was a microwave oven. It knocked him down, but he was up quick and out of there. Bill volunteered to take a turn, but Tango told him, that the power of the storm would knock him down, while he, on the other hand, could stand it.

Again, he noted, no brag, just fact.

Three

In the time that followed we further energized the city folk, many of whom had always thought the debris was a great god's odd turds.

At least that's what one of them told me. He could be the local bullshitter.

Tango helped the city folk make great ropes with hooks of wood, and then he convinced them to help him. What he did was he came to the great swirl and crawled on his belly over the wreckage, where the swirl was weakest, and fastened the hook to this or that, and then the city, and us—mostly I supervised—tugged items out of the swirl.

Tango set up shop right there, and as the days passed, he was able to fix the damaged wing and delight in the fact that there was fuel in the plane. It may have been pulled from an earlier time, but here in Down World it was Now, and the gas worked fine. The engine started, the propeller whirled. Of course, someone, and it wasn't going to be me, had to grab the propeller and give it a yank, and then be out of the way fast enough before it caught and began to spin. If you were too slow, it could be messy.

Tango and Suzie Q took it for a test flight, bumping it over rough ground, and finally taking to the sky. Up it went, soon to be the size of a dragonfly.

Tango told us to meet him and Suzie Q back at the city. He intended to land it there on one of the great plazas. When we arrived back and saw the plane sitting on the plaza near our cone house, we rejoiced.

We had a big feast and we invited everyone. Tango had killed several wild hogs and Suzie Q and Bill had gathered fruit. I was sent on a scouting mission to see what other foods could be found, but I spent a lot of that time in the cone house sleeping. I did this after I found a freshwater cistern I could swim in, though I suppose I should have suggested no one drink any water that came directly from that source for a while, as I had, and not meaning to, peed a little.

The feast was marvelous, cooked by Bill. The town folks only provided hungry mouths and clay jars of some sort of liquor. Oh, and some horns and drums. Tango said the drums looked like bongos.

Sometime after Bill had drank some of the liquor and insisted Suzie Q drink none, he took one of the bongos and began to beat it, and Tango, perhaps about six sheets to the wind, still wearing that ragged fleece, began to dance in a hopping style, lifting his head to the sky, letting out a wild jungle yell that made the fur on my back stand up and caused me to pass excited gas.

I drank only one small clay pot of the liquor, to wash the wild hog down with, and the next thing I knew I was waking up in the cone house with a headache.

But, from that time on, Tango called Bill, Bongo Bill, and so did we.

In short time we went back to the Time Swirl, and not long after we had big trucks that worked, and there was even a truck full of fuel, which Tango said supplied gasoline to filling stations.

The trucks, with much trouble, due to the terrain, were driven to the city, and though I can't say how much time it took, eventually we had six trucks. One was what Tango called a dump truck, the other was a trash truck, there was the fuel truck, and two small automobiles. Tango knocked out the windshields and mounted guns on their dashboards. The guns were taken from other fighter planes we discovered. The ammunition was sparse, so the training was all simulated, saving the ammo for the conflict. Of course, dry firing wasn't the best way to assure accuracy or even a true understanding of the weapons, but we did what we could with repeated aiming, trigger pulls and theoretical instruction.

I was of some good use, as my traveling with Wells had taught me much about machinery. I couldn't build a time machine from scratch, but I could repair or modify some of the things we found and make them better. I have a box of tools on my sled and some of the tools are sophisticated instruments. I also have a nice little toilet on the sled, but really, anything, number one or number two, drops out on the ground, so I guess there is a lack of sophistication there.

The city folk were about as resourceful as an extra asshole, but in time they began to want to help, which led to them mostly getting in the way.

We sent them on scouting missions.

Some had not left the city since birth, but out they went, some becoming lost right away, which meant Tango had to go find them, but in time they became better at their mission.

They came back and told of seeing the great army and the machines, and they had seen the fuzzy fat woman, and now she was less fuzzy than I had described. She was a slow-moving puddle of vibrating meat. Whatever she was, there appeared to be some kind of constant transformation.

The army was not right on top of us, it was reported, but they were not far away. With that news, Tango increased his concentration on rescuing Leo. The idea of it kept his mind off of Jill, not because it didn't matter, but because as he had deduced before, saving Leo was possible. He had done all he could for Jill, and it was his belief that it was his fault Leo had been captured.

It was the noble thing to do, and that gets me every time. It's like in the Dime Novels I read. Great and stupid gestures where everyone ended up being brave and ending up with their donkey in a ditch hit me deep in the soul.

That said, I considered making for the river and going on alone, away from this certain madness, but no matter how much logic told me I should do this, I stuck.

The scouting parties, now more assured, went out and came back with news. Four sleeps and the army would arrive. There were jungles to spoil and land to rape, and men and women to rape and murder, and then they could roll on. But to what purpose?

No one had an answer to that.

Tango Tells It Now

When the army was approximately two sleeps away, we could see them from our mountain perch. We could see the jungle going down before the machines, and we could see the head machine, a large thing with giant wheels and monstrous rollers, pulled and pushed by slaves. It covered a great patch of land, and that land was broken and flat and there were fires where the trees had been burned perhaps for cooking, but most likely for nothing other than happy destruction.

We had arrived at the city from the mountains and through the valley, but they had found another route, and it was a flatter and swifter route. I was glad, however, that we hadn't found it, otherwise we would have found them sooner than we were prepared, though I must admit, I didn't hold great hope for our preparation. I thought too that I might feel a bit self-destructive myself due the circumstances, Jill dying and me without a cure. Perhaps she was already dead.

But Leo lived, and it was my plan to rescue him, something that might last briefly before he, and all of us, were driven down and smashed flat. Watching them from our perch showed them to be fearsome and formidable.

I could not see Leo from there, but I could see the slaves and the army, a mass of movement, like ants in search of their hill. I hoped Leo was still alive. It would certainly have been ironic to discover he was already dead.

I felt bad as well, in that I seemed to have given the city hope. They thought they might be able to protect themselves and turn the tide of the attack. Of course, I hoped that as well, but the difference was the army coming had become battle-hardened. The army of the city had poked at straw targets and were still lucky to hit much with their bows and arrows, their spears. They used their swords like piñata sticks, exercising all the finesse of... Well, there wasn't any finesse.

We had found a trail that we could drive the trucks down on, and that trail would empty out onto the vast plain and would lead to the creature's army. I say creature due to descriptions. I didn't know what to call her. Ned says that it is a she.

The trick was to hit them in the field, and then use our clandestine, and certainly unique plans, to surprise and cripple them. If that didn't work, well, my friends and the city were butt-fucked and shit-wiped. I learned that from a colorful relative.

Ned and I fastened a battering ram of sorts on the front of the big trash truck, having decided to use it like a tank. I had taught Goseff to drive, mostly straight-line stuff. He can turn, but boy does he turn wide, so we try to save that maneuver for a last-minute tactic, if you could call it a tactic.

I have taught another, Wytot, to drive the dump truck. We filled the back of the truck, the dumpster part, with armed men with bows and arrows. We made ladders that are solid and fastened to the inside of the dumpster. They can stand at the top of the ladders and shoot arrows and throw spears. We have been working on those things with them, trying to return old knowledge to them about the use of the weapons in their warehouses. In some ways it saddens me to do that, but there is a saying I have adopted over the years from unhappy experience. "Have no army, have no home."

I plan to fly the bi-plane. In another existence in my long life I flew one in World War One and was shot down behind the lines, captured briefly by German soldiers. But that is another story. Let me say only, obviously, it worked out. I killed many, even while in captivity, which didn't last long. I made a long and daring escape across no man's land.

The plane I would fly here was actually a German plane from that war, a Fokker, the best of the heavier than air battle craft of the time. It was a double-wing plane, one of the earlier versions. I have painted it red with a paint made from clay and oil. It looks pretty good. I want to be seen. I want to strike fear into the hearts of the enemy with the blood-red plane. Also, it's a very nice bright sort of color. I have always liked red. The gun on the Fokker works, and there is quite a bit of ammunition there, as well as a revolver that was lying on the seat. I wonder what the story is there. Carved into the pistol's hilt is G8. I have an idea who the pistol belonged to, but again, this is not the place for that discussion.

We have mounted a gun on our zeppelin made of tight webbing and gassy plants. We have borrowed an engine and propeller from another plane that was mostly destroyed, and we have attached it to the floating device, and we have tried it. It works well. Ned will fly the zeppelin using the plane motor. There is also a gun mounted so that it fires at the right moment when the propeller turns. It's a very exact science, but it's one I learned in WW1.

Ned and I have attached a gas dump underneath the zeppelin. Gas we took from the gas truck. It couldn't have been in the pile long. Pulling it out with a winch and lots of workers and some oxen the city had was quite a chore. But it was worth it. It has provided gasoline for our vehicles and gas for the gas dump under the zeppelin. That is a risky plan, but it is a plan. We'll see if it works.

Also in the zeppelin are squirming bags of spiders and snakes. They make Ned nervous, but he is on board with our plan to use them. We need every distraction we can manage.

The problem is, except for me and Ned, the others are not drivers of cars or any other kind of vehicle, though Bongo Bill has some minor experience. He had just gotten his license on his earth, but mostly went by the metal trees or public transport. He drives like an old man with bad eyesight. Still, he will get by. He has to.

Suzie Q is such a whiz with the bow and arrow, better than me— and that means something—I will place her in position to best use the bow to air our attack. She and some of the others will go by steamboat down the river and come up from the side. Their actions will be guerrilla assaults.

Guerrilla makes me think of gorilla, and from there I jump to apes. As for the apes. They have not been seen. I had high hopes that Rotah and her tribe would come to help us. But then again, I hadn't planned on, or prepared her to participate in a war.

I gathered our warriors on the large stone plaza and stood up on the bi-plane. I gave a speech, said how unlikely our survival might be, suggested they all melt into the jungle and hide out, but none in the city would. They had found their spine and they had found their purpose. Protect their city. Rebuild.

I doubt either would be a success, but I told them that, so that is off my conscience.

As for Ned and Suzie Q and Bongo Bill, I told them personally that I saw little to no purpose in their involvement, as Leo was my friend, and they had never met him, and for that matter, Jill was my concern as well, and as for the others, well, they were trying to protect their city and rebuild a better way of life. They had a dog in that fight.

Like the city's would-be warriors, I gave them a ticket out. But Ned wrote on his slate for all of them.

WE ARE IN.

After teaching a very capable woman named Mulax to drive the steamboat, she and Suzie Q and others packed the boat and started away. But not before Suzie Q and Bongo Bill said their goodbyes to one another.

"She is only a child," Bongo Bill said when she was gone.

"You should have made her stay, and then leave, find some place to hide in the jungle."

"You've never had a little sister, have you?"

"Only an ape sister. You could say I was adopted."

"Did she do as you asked?"

"Not at all."

"Then you know."

The army was near to the city, and our army was as ready as it was going to be. I went over the plans once more with those who would be executing them, leading others, and the talking was done.

I was about to climb into the bi-plane and prepare for take-off, using a long section of the plaza as a runway. I wore the fleece around my neck, gently tied, and easily removable with a grab at the knot. I had on a loin cloth that was made from a stretch of bright red cloth; it was my war uniform. I had a bow and a quiver of arrows with me. The gun mounted on the plane would be my best bet, but I liked to go old school for comfort. Of course, I had a knife strapped to my waist.

Ned was soon to use his sled to enter the zeppelin, but at that moment he was beside me on the ground.

He wrote on his slate.

I AM CURIOUS ABOUT SOMETHING.

"And what would that be, little friend?"

WHERE DID ALL THE PEOPLE GO THAT WERE IN THE MACHINES WE HAVE?

"No idea, Ned. But it's my belief that when that time whirl comes, it pulls the machines through but destroys human flesh and bone. There were no skeletons, no rotting bodies, and the machines came from many places and times. There had to be people in at least some of them when the Time Twist took the machines away. I can't explain it."

OK. DON'T GET KILLED.

"Same to you, Ned. And no matter what our outcome, it has been an honor knowing you."

YEAH. YOU'RE RIGHT. I AM SPECIAL.

An Omniscient Aside

And the trucks rolled and the zeppelin lifted and the bi-plane buzzed. The steamboat was almost near its destination. An army of ragged citizens dressed in the armor and carrying the weapons of their ancestors marched forward.

Now it is time to show the battle.

Later, after Ned had many other adventures, a short silent film serial was made of this adventure. It appeared in the 1930s in one of the American time lines. It showed in twelve parts. It was written by Ned himself. It was not believed to be a true story, though Ned insisted that it was, at least it was before the Hollywood writers "punched it up".

The serial was called TANGO AND NED. A man in a seal suit played Ned. A man too big to travel through trees, far bigger than Tango, played Tango. Big as that man was, Tango could have wadded him into a ball and shot a hoop with him.

Of course, basketball was nowhere near as popular then as it became.

This adventure, TANGO AND NED, was a comic strip before it was a film. It appeared in black and white in the dailies, and in color on Sundays. There were different artists. Both were good.

It was a Pulp Novel before it was a comic strip. Ned never did write it up as a Dime Novel, though he did go back in time and do that with other stories. In the pulp the story was titled TANGO AND NED DOWN UNDER. It had a painting of a German Fokker on the cover. In the front cockpit was Ned the Seal firing a machine gun, and in the back seat, piloting the craft, for it was done from that position, was Tango.

This cover representation wasn't in the story, because Ned was not in the Fokker when the event happened. The artist thought it made a good cover, though, and it did. The magazine, FIGHTING AIR STORIES, is very collectable, and that issue even more collectable. Of course, not all the action in the story took place in the air.

It was a true story, printed as fiction. It was certainly embellished.

One thing could be said, and was said, the story in all its mediums stayed pretty much the same, taking into consideration that other writers always had to fuck it up a little to bring in their own versions. This was primarily the film serial version. The screenwriters who rewrote Ned decided changes would make it a better story. Their own thoughts they felt were better than the original. Ned even got some starlet pussy in a patched-in scene that took place before Ned took to the air. Implied, not shown. It was an earlier and supposedly more innocent time. They made the viewers aware by the man in the seal suit strutting about after an encounter in a dark shed. Not showing it was supposed to make it somehow less offensive, as if the imagination didn't do that anyway.

But a seal and a starlet? A seal that walked like a man in an ill-fitting suit with a shiny zipper on the side?

What the hell? Why would a seal and a human—

Never mind.

Let's recap.

There was a comic strip, written by Ned. Fine art by Jack Kirby.

TANGO AND NED was a pulp story. Ned wrote this one.

It was a stage play. Ned co-wrote this one with his friend Eugene O'Neill, who also co-wrote with Ned *THE ICE MAN COMETH*, which was about an encounter with an Abominable Snowman and how it changed people's lives, made them better, or destroyed them. The Ice Man ends up working in America driving an ice delivery truck. Delivered ice was a big thing then. The play was very existential. Ned sometimes suggested that he wrote nearly all of it and that O'Neill only added a few elements here and there. This is a subject of debate.

Later, a 3-D version film was considered. Didn't happen.

It was always called TANGO AND NED, or TANGO AND NED DOWN UNDER, no matter what other versions were made. Other than a shorter novel that Ned wrote about his time on Mars, called NED THE SEAL ON MARS, it was the most popular of his stories. Thus, all the different versions.

In the far future, in the same time line, there will be a musical. The part of the seal will actually be played by Ned, and at this point in time he will have an actual voice, though his ability to hit low notes was not heralded. For that matter, neither were the rest of his notes.

Even farther in the future it will be a mind-story plugged into the head. In that version, you may choose to play certain roles yourself, from hero to villain; you can even be Ned or Tango. You will be able to see, smell, taste, and feel the adventure. Whatever you feel, including wounds, decapitations, castrations, and stomach misery, will pass.

Nov. 5th — TEN UNUSUAL STORIES

ARGOSY

10¢

WEEKLY

A SHORT INTERMISSION FOLLOWS
SNACK BAR IS OPEN.
TOILETS ARE CLEAN.

Part Three:

The battle begins. There is a battle from the air. There are arrows in the air. There are deaths. Snakes and spiders, oh my. There is a primate surprise. Leo is found. Things get nasty. And a little later, one big fucking surprise.

On Film

Remember the film serial. Let's talk about that a bit.

On one alternate world Ned became a film buff and wanted to direct, and possibly star in film. Now and again, he saw the world as if it were a film.

His first experience with film, a Pippo the Hippo cartoon and a news reel, along with a serial chapter, forever affected him.

In the moments when the battle between the Golden Fleece Army and the Army of She Who Must Be Obeyed and Eats Lunch Early began, Ned, without meaning to, saw it all as a film, and later he would script, direct, and have a part in the film, though he railed at having his script revised and rewritten in spots by the producer's chosen rewriters.

He called them those ham-handed bastards.

But the events were happening then in his head. He couldn't help it. After seeing early silent films, he was hooked, and in the back of his mind, even as it was happening for real, he envisioned it for reel.

FILM SERIAL, TANGO AND NED, EPISODE EIGHT: THE BATTLE

BLACK AND WHITE

The film is a bit jittery in Ned's head, like the first moving pictures he saw. It was something like this:

FADE IN:

ESTABLISH THE SKY

A constant sun. A puff of fast-blowing clouds.

A German bi-plane. A Fokker, to be exact.

We can see the pilot. His scarf; in this case it's a ragged golden fleece. It flaps behind him like a cape, well, it is a cape. It flaps and the pilot drives. Ned is not in the plane. As mentioned before, that was added by the all-knowing film folk.

CLOSE ON PILOT

He's handsome. It's TANGO THE MONKEY MAN.

AERIAL VIEW OF THE GROUND

The plane's shadow cruising over the earth.

The earth is covered in jungle, but the jungle is falling before something we HEAR, but only glimpse.

WIDEN

A BIG GODDAMN ARMY

It's practically a walking city. Amongst the walkers, machines.

CLOSE ON THE LEAD MACHINE

It is enormous, made of stone and wood and weird metal and possibly plastic, or something akin to it, stolen from a flying saucer.

Slaves are pulling and pushing the machine, but it's not because it doesn't have power of its own. That's in reserve. We'll find out more about that later.

Emaciated slaves are falling out. The army walks over them. Machines roll over them. Even the slaves walk over them.

WIDE VIEW

BAD ARMY'S POV

What's in front of them? A field. To their left and right, jungle, and many of the balloon trees, their bright pods floating and fluttering in the wind. A few pods are breaking loose of the limbs that hold them, floating upwards.

HIGH ON A HILL

A blue stone city, white plazas, shining bright in the constant high-noon sunlight.

REAR VIEW OF THE BAD ARMY

Devastation. Smashed trees. Smoke drifts. Gouged earth. Slave bodies littered here and there like discarded refuse, many of them flat as bath mats.

CUT TO:

A CLOSE-UP OF THE BIG-ASS MACHINE

It creaks and moans as if it is a living thing. It rolls and crunches and steam rolls from the back of it. No source for the steam is seen.

CLOSER YET ON THE MACHINE'S ONLY RIDER

A blob. Maybe it's a woman. And maybe… Well, maybe it's a blob. Red-eyed, and the eyes pop with electricity. Smoke plumes from her mouth where jagged black teeth, like oily, wrecked machine cogs, reside.

Her body pulses. There is something inside of her.

ANOTHER ANGLE ON THIS MONSTER

Let's make it a side view.

Oh, hell. This is one nasty-looking beast. Worms crawl in, worms crawl out. She is nude but there is nothing sexual about her. Her breasts are like airless rubber rafts, her vagina is like a monstrous wound. One leg becomes thin near the bottom. The foot is small, unlike the other foot, which is balloon-like with fat peanut-shaped toes.

The heel of the small foot is bleeding, and we can see it throb.

ANOTHER ANGLE ON THE VAST FIELD

We see the army of the Golden Fleece coming. They wear armor and are armed, but they march like they have all been given different directions. Their armor hangs like hobo suits.

One of the soldiers, a woman with too-large, clattering armor, leads a sudden charge. They rush at the much larger army commanded by the Fat Thing.

It's a noble gesture, but it looks about as promising as trying to fill in the Grand Canyon with a spoon and a beach bucket.

ON THE FAT THING

It lifts its fingers and blue-white electricity (we will have this in color in our minds) bolts out of her fingers and across the field, hits the advancing army, knocks the Golden Fleece warriors ass over sandals, sets them on fire.

ON THE WOMAN LEADER

She is hit and down and cooking in her armor like a crab in a pot of boiling water. We see her only briefly.

ANOTHER VIEW POINT

A vast expanse of the battlefield.

Dead smoking Golden Fleece warriors that look like burning sticks and blackened rags.

ANGLE ON SHE'S ARMY

We see the slaves pulling and pushing machines. They are wasted figures.

ON ONE OF THEM

A black man. This is LEO. He looks stronger than the rest, healthier than the rest, but he's got a wobble to him.

ZEPPELIN'S EYE VIEW

Well, zeppelin of sorts, but we're seeing down from it.

AND NOW WE'RE ON THE ZEPPELIN

The zeppelin is the vast net filled with gas plants, and underneath the netting there is a motor house. It is essentially a box with an open front for the operator to see where he is going. Side windows, and one at the rear. There is no glass, just cutaways for the windows.

Below the motor house is a large tree trunk, hollowed out and plugged on both ends, but one end has a rope fastened to it, and the rope runs up and into the bottom of the motor house.

A propeller at the back of the motor house beats at the air, pushing the zeppelin forward.

Lots of dark smoke coming out of the rear of the little motor house, and we glimpse a driver through a side window, but we can't see clearly who it is. Not yet.

And then—

CLOSER—

AS SEEN THROUGH THE CRUDE CUT-OUT SIDE WINDOW IN THE ZEPPELIN

GO CLOSE ON NED THE SEAL

He looks to be in intense thought. His mouth is moving, but we can't hear him. He's working a crude steering wheel that looks as if it's been salvaged from an automobile.

NOW WE ARE EVEN CLOSER ON NED, BUT INSIDE THE ZEPPELIN

PLACARD CARD

It shows us what Ned is thinking. All the placards are slates like the one Ned carries on a cord around his neck.

We can see that Ned is singing inside his head. His mouth isn't moving, but we get the idea, though we can't actually hear him. Part of this is due to there being musical notes to indicate what is going on, and the close view of his head which gives the impression of internal knowledge.

NED'S CARD
Oh, I'm a seal. I'm a bad-ass seal.
I'm on a mission. Hope I don't get killed.
I got a gun. I got ammo.
Gonna drop bombs. Whammo.
I don't know. That's not much of a battle song.
Ned the Seal forever.
No. That doesn't say much.
Man. I'm hungry. I need some dried fish.
I packed some somewhere.
Eyes on the wheel.
Get a book on rhymes.

EXT. THE ZEPPELIN

As we—

CUT TO:

THE BATTLEFIELD, AIR AND GROUND, AS IT HAPPENS

CAMERA PLAYS HERE, THEN THERE, AND WE SEE A SERIES OF ACTION MOMENTS

...the armies collide, and it's not looking good for the Golden Fleece team. They go down faster than two-dollar hookers (male or female) at Mardi Gras.

And then the Golden Fleece team breaks apart to allow the arrival of Goseff in the big-ass garbage truck, a partner sitting on the passenger side, gun taken from the Time Whirl mounted on the dash, sticking out where the window used to be, firing over the hood of the truck, knocking down the bad guys with meaty impact and sprays of blood (the color of ink in this black and white film).

IN THE AIR, ON TANGO

Tango dives the Fokker, starts firing.

THE GROUND

There is so much confusion, some of the slaves bite it. Bullets smack near Leo. The slaves start to make a run for it, but the army beats them back into position with whips and pokes of swords and spears.

BACK TO TANGO

Tango finishes his machine gun strafing, lifts the Fokker skyward, and in that moment—

ON LEO

And in that moment of confusion, he snatches a spear from one of the tormentors, stabs him through the throat, and makes a break for it.

ON THE SHE-ARMY

The army is involved now in trying to dodge the garbage truck as it smashes through their lines.

GO TO LEO

As he makes a running escape toward the jungle.

Arrows zip past him like bees.

ON GOSEFF AND HIS GARBAGE TRUCK

Spears and arrows and stones whirled by slings strike through the open truck window.

ANGLE ON GOSEFF

An arrow nails Goseff in the eye. He loses control of the truck. It veers wild, smashing the attacking army's soldiers, slaves, everything in its path.

ANOTHER ANGLE

As the truck, out of control, hits She's machine. It's like a jetting bee smashing into a brick wall. The truck bounces back, flips over, spins, takes out a row of slaves which have been forced to the front of the lines as a shield, slides and comes to a ground-gouging stop.

FRONT WINDOW OF UPSIDE DOWN TRUCK

As the machine gunner crawls bloodied and broken out of the front window, trying to get up, trying to make a run for it.

A SHADOW

It's the BIG MACHINE

It rolls over him and the truck, driving them into the ground. As the Big Machine rolls away, all that is left is a flat sheet of metal and a greasy spot where the gunner had been.

CUT TO:

NED

We see him looking out of the side window of his machine.

INT. ZEPPELIN

Ned, pulling at the throttle, drifting the craft to the right.

SHADOW OF THE ZEPPELIN ON THE BATTLEFIELD

It's over one of the smaller rolling machines.

There is a clutch of warriors with bows and arrows on the platform at the top of the machine.

Widen to include slaves pulling and pushing the machine. They look up at the shadow.

ON NED

He has a flipper and thumb out the window, and that flipper and thumb are holding a squirming bag.

Ned lets the bag drop.

FOLLOW THAT BAG DOWN

It is coming open even as it drops.

A snake wiggles out, falls.

The bag strikes the top portion of the machine, and out fly and crawl and writhe all manner of snakes. One of them strikes at a surprised warrior's legs.

CLOSE ON ITS HEAD AND FANGS

As they bury deep.

BACK TO SCENE

The falling snake wraps around a warrior's head. It strikes, fanging the warrior in the neck.

Other warriors are panicking, leaping off the machine's platform to their death or injury. Some end up being rolled over by the machine. A squirt of wet darkness splashes out from beneath the machine.

ANOTHER ANGLE ON THE GROUND

One of the warriors who leaped manages to rise to his feet, but one leg is gone. A bone sticks out of it. He wobbles and falls.

Slaves slip their harnesses. They swarm the injured warrior, begin to kick and punch him. Soon they swarm him like flies on shit.

ANOTHER VIEW OF THE FLYING ZEPPELIN

The hollow log beneath it.

INT. ZEPPELIN

Ned grins, yanks at a gear.

EXT. ZEPPELIN, BELOW THE MOTOR HOUSE

As the log drops down in front and the plug is jerked from it by a rope, and out rolls gasoline.

GASOLINE SPRAYING WIDE ACROSS THE SKY

ON THE BIG MACHINE

As She Who Must Be Obeyed and Eats Lunch Early looks up.

Down comes the gas, soaking her misshapen body as she sits in the open machine.

ON HER FACE

A frown crawls across her wide mouth; it looks more like a rip in fabric.

EXT. EDGE OF THE JUNGLE

As Leo enters into the foliage.

ANOTHER ANGLE

There is a slope in the jungle, and below it we see the river, and on the river we see the steamboat, and coming down a gangplank from boat to shore are a handful of folks, and one of them is Suzie Q carrying her bow, and Bongo Bill is with her.

Leo sees them, startles.

POV OF BOAT FOLK

They are looking up at Leo.

ON BONGO BILL

Placard card comes up as he speaks.

                    BONGO BILL

          Leo, I presume.

BACK TO SCENE

A happy Leo, as he realizes they are not the enemy. But he still looks cautious.

WIDEN SCENE TO INCLUDE BOAT FOLK AND LEO

They are closer together now.

ON BONGO BILL

His placard card now.

> BONGO BILL
> We are friends of Tango.

ANGLE ON LEO

Leo's placard card.

> LEO
> Thank goodness.

BACK TO THE BATTLE

ON NED IN THE ZEPPELIN

His placard card shows what he's thinking.

> NED
> Where the fuck is Suzie Q and Bongo Bill?

ANGLE NED

He is throwing more bags out. They open as they fall.

Spiders float. Snakes drop.

THE BATTLEFIELD

Spiders land in the hair and on the bodies of She's warriors. They jump and dance.

Snakes smack and explode, but some live, and they crawl through the ranks, striking wildly.

Open mouths of warriors as they silently scream and slap at spiders or kick at snakes.

THE EMPTY SKY

Arrows flying up.

ANOTHER ANGLE AS—

Arrows strike the bottom of the zeppelin.

ANOTHER VIEW

Arrows shooting through the gaps in the net, popping gas plants.

AS THE GAS PLANTS DEFLATE

The zeppelin begins to spin and starts to swirl downward, toward She's Bad Army.

ON THE BAD ARMY

They are looking up at the spinning craft.

They look happy. One of the soldiers licks his lips.

INT. ZEPPELIN

Ned frantically working the gear, trying to gain control of his falling craft as the zeppelin and motor house spin.

NED'S CARD
(what he's thinking)
Shit.

CUT TO A PLACARD CARD

CARD
Is this the end of the plucky seal? Will he
just be so much busted blubber?

Tune in next week for the stirring climax to TANGO AND NED.

LIGHTS OUT ON CHAPTER EIGHT

Leo and Other Stuff

When Leo arrived at the river, two apes and a clutch of armed warriors greeted him.

He was surprised that they recognized him, as he had never met any of the group, and felt he would have remembered two armed apes, but when they explained that they were friends of Tango, it all fell into place.

"We must reach the battlefield," the ape that introduced himself as Bongo Bill said.

Leo turned and pointed up the hill.

"You may rest on the boat," Bongo Bill said.

"Give me a spear, or a sword," Leo said. "Anything. I'm going with you."

A spear was provided.

"We are sneaking," said the young ape, who was armed with the bow and a quiver of arrows and appeared to be a female.

"We'll start at the edge of the jungle," Bongo Bill said.

———⊷⊶———

Meantime, back at the battlefield, and a smidgeon earlier.

One

From the Journal of Ned the Seal

I knew that if I didn't act fast, I would land in the middle of the battle-field. There were enough un-popped gas plants to bring the motor house to a landing without too much impact, but being in the middle of the battlefield, trapped beneath a mesh of withering plants wouldn't be a good place for a handsome little seal like myself to be.

But it seemed unavoidable.

Worse yet, I had coated that big-ass hunk of meat on the giant rolling machine with gasoline, but our plan to follow that procedure with another had not been implemented.

Bongo Bill and, most importantly, Suzie Q had not arrived.

As I gripped my stun rod and made plans to give my life dearly, the motor house made impact with the ground.

It was some landing.

I was knocked off my sled, where I had been positioned, looking out the front window, such as it was. The jarring impact was more than I had planned for, as there were still a large number of gas plants intact.

I lay there for a moment, not exactly sure what had happened, where I was, or who I was, when I heard a motor humming. I thought at first that it was the motor of my own machine, but no, that was dead on impact. This was an outside motor.

I wriggled back onto my sled, feeling all my bruises, and looked out the front window, which was the direction where the noise was the loudest.

Landing in front of my wrecked craft was the Fokker and Tango was looking over at me, waving his arm for me to come.

I lifted the sled, and managed my way out of the front window of the wheelhouse, jetted toward the parked Fokker, the propeller spinning, bathing me in hot air as I approached. Tango waved for me to hasten to him, as if he thought I might stop to examine an anthill or pause to take a dump.

A wave of the Bad Army warriors were descending on us. There was one in the lead, carrying a spear. He didn't have experience with airplane propellers, and what experience he would soon gain wouldn't help him in the future.

He walked right into the propeller and disappeared in a swirl of mangled flesh, shattered bone, and spraying blood. It was kind of pretty, if you didn't think about the source.

I made it to the Fokker, used my sled to lift to the empty front seat, and tried to glide the sled into it, but the sled was too large.

I pushed it over the side with regret, and took my place in the seat. Tango maneuvered the plane about, and started racing over the battlefield.

As we rose and turned in the air, still low to the ground, Tango yelled for me to operate the machine gun. I grabbed at the firing device mounted in front of me and began to fire as Tango went low and headed over the battlefield.

It was a kind of horrible feeling, holding that trigger device down, having the gun fire rapidly and scatter bodies across the field, cutting them in pieces as surely as the propeller had that warrior.

I feared I might hit some of the slaves, as there was a riot going on, and the slaves had turned on their masters during the confusion. Up until now the Bad Army had used their machines and army size to walk right over their foes, but we had implements that they had not imagined, and it had given us a tactical advantage. At least for the moment. This tactical advantage included the dump truck, which was racing about the battlefield. The warriors inside the bed, strapped to the side with ropes, were firing arrows.

And now another part of the plan was put into action. The cars with the mounted guns came racing onto the battlefield, driven as if by madmen. They slid on the field and one even spun completely around, and that wasn't intentional, I can say with certainty.

Those mounted guns took out a bunch of the Bad Army, not to mention a horde of slaves who were in the wrong spot at the wrong time.

The Golden Fleece Army was well onto the field now, working in better form than they had at first, taking on seasoned warriors with great panache. I just learned that word, and hope that was the place to use it. Even their sword work looked remarkably better. The lessons Tango had taught them had finally kicked in.

Just as it looked as if the tide was turning in our favor, just as Tango turned the plane in anticipation of another run across the battlefield, the Fat One activated her machine with some yet unseen power, wheeled it, crushing several of her own army folk under its rollers, and began churning in the direction of the descending Fokker.

This was an unexpected trick. That damn machine had its own power, could operate without slaves and draft animals. Perhaps it was power that needed to be preserved, but the bottom line was it was racing over the battlefield like a spotted-ass ape (they are very fast).

As Tango fired and the Fat One received the bullets, they went through her like flies through smoke. If she was hurt, it didn't show. It was a little like poking a finger through dough.

She stood up in front of her seat and held out her hands and shot out writhing blue bolts of electricity that struck the Fokker's propeller and caused it to whine loudly like a boy with his dick caught in a zipper. The propeller came loose of the airplane, whipped off and down onto the battlefield, along with my fez, stolen by the wind. I noted that the propeller was chopping through friend and foe alike on the ground.

A tip. Without a propeller, a plane doesn't fly so well. Within moments the Fokker was skidding nose first into the dirt. It flipped and the tail rose high and I was tossed way out and came down painfully skidding on my belly right in front of the great rolling machine, the Fat One looking down on me like a crow that's just spotted a worm. She and her machine were so close, I could smell the gasoline that I had coated the machine and her with.

Seals are not made for dry land, as you most likely know, so I was scootching along with considerable desperation, if not great speed. The wheels came closer. I looked up and knew my time had come. In moments, I would be seal jelly.

Two

The wheels rolled over me and I was killed immediately.

Ha. Just fucking with you.

Tango appeared out of nowhere, snatched me up and tossed me away from the grinding wheels, causing me to skid again on my belly, scraping me badly, but compared to what had been about to happen, was nothing more than an inconvenience.

One bit of excellent news, outside of my having been tossed from the rolling damnation that was about to befall me, my fez was lying right in front of me. I reached out and put it on and looked back as the machine reached Tango.

Let me tell you. I do not know how he did it, but he leaped, practically flat-footed, and caught the bottom of the Fat One's seat, swung himself up and onto her perch, his golden fleece cape flapping in the wind. He punched her in the belly hard enough to cause an elephant to pass gas, but it had no effect on her. A sternly written note in invisible ink would have been about as effective.

She slapped him with a backhand movement. As she did her fingers lit up with electric fire, and there were flicks of flame and smoke in Tango's hair when he fell beside the machine, landing hard, face down.

No one else human might have withstood that, but Tango did, and before you could say it "Looks like our shit is mixed with gravel", he was up and climbing the side of the machine. Before going up, he had stuck his knife between his teeth, and the eternal sunlight made the blade wink as if his mouth were filled with metal teeth.

Fat One must have thought Tango was done, for she was concentrating on the dump truck now, shooting out bolts from her fingers, hot strikes from her eyes. The surges hit the dump truck full of warriors and electrified it. The heads sticking up over the side of the dump truck smoked and the skulls popped and the truck was kicked up in the air, came down and rolled on its side, flinging blackened, smoking bodies every which way.

Tango had made the summit of the machine, and was now striking at the Fat One with his knife. I saw it go up and go down as he sprang to the top of her head and threw his bronzed legs over her shoulders.

Then the machine whirled and I could only see Tango's back as he sat perched on the Fat One's shoulders, his knife going up and down like a rabbit dick fucking a doe.

(Female rabbits are called does. Some information I thought you might like to have.)

Three

A burst of glaring electrical energy, blue-white and lingering, You could have lit up New York and a small, reasonably populated town with that power.

Tango was once again thrown from the machine and once again his hair smoked and he was lit up like a rich man's Christmas tree. His golden fleece cape caught on fire and disappeared in a burst of flaming wool and charcoal-colored smoke.

And this time when he struck the ground, he didn't move.

From way on high I saw a flaming arrow dipping toward the Fat One's rolling machine, which was easily crushing a wad of Golden Fleece warriors beneath its rollers. The arrow went right through the fat one's head, but the fire on it stayed with her gas-coated self and the flames from it spread immediately to the gas-coated machine. The machine and its operator were engulfed in fire.

The Fat One fell off the machine, hit the dirt, and stood, the flames licking around her like a hungry dog trying to get the goods out of an open can of meat.

Fat One stutter-stepped and then stopped and turned her blazing head to the stationary sun and let out a yell, and at that very moment, out of the jungle came a great army of apes, brandishing clubs and stones.

The apes lit into the Bad Army so fast there wasn't time for them to even perceive what was happening. It must have felt like a dark dream.

The apes clubbed them and struck them with their fists, threw them and bit them.

As for the blazing Fat One, she staggered a couple more steps, then collapsed onto her belly. Flames rolled over her and she exploded into a mass of hot, wet meat, some of which landed on me and burned my skin a little. I can show you the scar later if you'd like to look.

Fat One opened her mouth and great bolts of lightning burped out of it, and then the lightning died. Her head cracked like a sun-soaked watermelon and dark things came out, strange, shadowy shapes that looked like the aliens we had seen in the underwater saucer. The shapes twisted and moved and became one and then there were pops of electricity and the electricity joined the cloud of alien forms floating over the fractured head of Fat One.

For a moment, her body had its own thunderstorm hovering above it. Then out of that came a spectral shape that at one moment resembled a swirl of smoke, and in another a red-furred ape-girl. All the ghostly images joined together, and with a pop, became a quick, singular lick of flame and then the flame guttered out. The air turned clear over Fat One's corpse and it was as if a weight of gloom had been lifted from the field.

———◆———

The apes had a bit of trouble distinguishing friend from foe. A few Golden Fleece warriors were dispatched by the apes during the confusion, but it was all soon sorted out. It wasn't a perfect ending to a dreadful day, but the opposite outcome would have deprived you of this excellent report on the battle, as it would have ended with me and the other dead warriors be prepared for supper.

In short, the apes and the Golden Fleece army soon made short work of the Bad Army, the bulk of which started running, making paths into the jungle that a monkey couldn't go.

The vats of oil, or tar, ended up being set on fire by flaming arrows, many of them launched by Suzie Q. The fires from these vats spread to the wagons that held them. They were turned to cinders within moments, and unfortunately, so were many of the draft animals, though some were saved.

In the end, we had taken only a few captives, as the apes were not in a sparing mood. It was all we could do to keep the former slaves from tearing the prisoners apart or beating them to death with rocks.

I will also admit here a dark moment.

Leo walked onto the battlefield, found the one he would later say was called General Joog. General Joog was trying to hide under the belly of an ox. The ox kept stepping on him, so that wasn't working out anyway.

Leo pulled him out from under the animal, by grabbing Joog's foot. What occurred after that was ugly. Let me just say an eye was lost and a neck was broken, and neither eye nor neck belonged to Leo.

Right at that moment, when I feared the worst for Tango, he managed to his feet, as if being erected by slow-moving machinery. His hair smoked in spots. His chest was scraped pink with blood. His loin cloth smoked a little. He looked at me, showed me a shine of teeth.

I held up one of my flippers, gave him a thumb's-up.

I'm proud of that grafted thumb, and never prouder of it than right at that moment.

I looked over to the edge of the jungle, and coming my way were Bongo Bill and Suzie Q, carrying her bow, a quiver of arrows rattling at her back.

As they reached me, Tango also arrived. He picked me up, held me in his arms. The whites of his eyes were red and he smelled like an outdoor barbecue, but overall, he looked all right.

Tango smiled at Suzie Q. "That was some shot, girl. Your flaming arrow ended the war."

"I never miss," she said. "If it's true, it's not brag, you know."

Tango laughed, then turned his attention to me.

"Hang on, little seal," he said, and carried me off the battlefield. He did that with ease, but I could tell that he wasn't quite his old self. He stumbled a little.

I really wasn't hurt that bad, but I let him carry me nonetheless. I was tired.

Four

The next few days were spent picking up bodies and burying them. Nobody was eaten for a change.

I got my sled back. It wasn't damaged in any significant way. Just bent up a bit here and there. I honked the horn to make sure it was working, and it was. The others seemed to think this was a pity. They have no sense of humor or feelings of simple joy.

There was a great feast to celebrate the victory, and a new head council was picked by the city to replace the brave and unfortunate Goseff. The city was damn proud of itself.

We remained there for some time, me and Tango healing our wounds. Fish was not served at any point during our convalescence, and that was a pity. We discovered that Tango could, at least for a while, light up one of the bulbs from a headlight from the remains of the dump truck. All he had to do was touch it and the headlamp glowed.

That was just for a while. In time, the ability passed. That was a good thing. When it was gone, Tango felt better. He claimed that for a bit, when he took a dump, his turds sizzled in the dirt. I don't know if he was joking or not.

Suzie Q and Bongo Bill were uninjured. They were our guerrillas, shooting arrows and such from the sidelines, so they hadn't been in the thick of it. Next time I want to fight from the sidelines, or maybe just draw up plans and point.

Leo mainly needed good food and rest. He came around quickly, and helped out nursing me and Tango.

While me and Tango convalesced, the others spent their time gathering supplies for a reverse trip down the river, and then an overland hike.

The apes lounged about for a few sleeps, became bored, and one moment they were there, and the next they were not. Except for Rohah. She decided she liked Bongo Bill. Really liked him. I think they did the nasty a few times. Before the apes left she appointed a new leader, and away they went. They weren't long on goodbyes or sentimentality. They took Bongo Bill's mess kit with them when they left. They knew a bit about cooking now.

Before they departed, they left fruit in front of the cone-shaped house where Suzie Q and Bongo Bill were staying, and they did the same in front of the house where Tango and my own seal self were recuperating. One piece of the fruit had a bite out of it. Bongo Bill said Burnt Toe had decided to have a bit of a taste before he departed. I had no idea which one of them was Burnt Toe.

In time, we were ready to go, but before our departure we had a kind of going-away party. A lot of food was served, no fish, however, and trumpets were blown. Bongo Bill beat on a makeshift bongo he had made. Bongo Bill had gotten good on those things, but the trumpets the city folk were hooting on were nothing more than a noise that made my fur stand up on my back like a pincushion full of needles. I honked my sled horn to help drown out their racket, and thought it sounded far better than their racket. Leo was the only one among us that could sing, and sing he did; blues songs and such, with everyone else singing along poorly, or like the Down World folk, just making accompaniment noise.

We eventually made our way down to the river and the steamboat, and many of the city folk followed after us. When our supplies and selves were loaded onto the boat, they threw flowers on the water, sang to us in a tuneless whine and waved to us, and tooted on those awful trumpets. I beeped my horn a lot, and before long we were out of their sight and sound and Tango promised to kill me if I honked my horn one more time.

I was tempted, but I let it remain silent.

Five

That trip was miserable for Tango. He was gloomy, and seemed less confident than his normal self. It was as if his ego had fallen off a shelf. He had set out to find the Golden Fleece, and had discovered it was just a skin and that its healing powers were so much malarkey.

On top of that, the skin itself, which was at least a sign that he had completed his quest, had been flame-dusted into nonexistence.

Yep. Tango felt so low he could have walked under a snake's belly wearing high heels.

There's not much to tell after that. We stuck to the river most of the trip, and there were a few close calls with dinosaurs, and we did encounter some water creatures that looked a lot like mermaids. As a seal, I knew of sea stories, but I had always thought mermaids were unlikely. But, we all felt we had seen them, if only from a distance. They didn't look like beautiful women at all. They looked wrinkled and scraggly-haired, ugly even from a distance where they were sunning on rocks. The wind carried their smell to us, and even I, who like a good spoiled herring, found their odor strong enough to knock over an elephant in a gas mask.

We all threw up from the stench, and I decided that smelling like something beyond dead and rotten was their super power.

Finally, we parked the steamboat, which we had rechristened, at least amongst ourselves, as the Odyssey. We left it on the shore by the city where the sleeping Jill either still lay asleep, or had been buried or cremated or snacked on. Tango assured me the latter was not at all likely. He said they were a different breed of folks, but I had learned over time that you can't really trust humans to be consistent when stress or hunger shows up. But there was also the fact that Tango might kill all of them, eat them, and shit them off a cliff. So, that could have been a deterrent.

As we neared the city, we saw fields of crops, lush with vegetables, talk stalks of corn and cane, blister-red tomatoes, yellow and green gourds, dangling purple beans, and vegetables I didn't recognize.

There were orchards full of fruit, and long paths made up of flat stone. It wasn't quite as unique as the city of the Golden Fleece, but it was certainly thriving better.

As we were entering the city, we saw sentries posted at stone sentry houses, but they neither spoke to us nor tried to stop us. All that happened was a runner came out of one of the sentry houses and darted up the road as if his pants were on fire.

Well, he wasn't wearing pants. He had on a loin cloth, but you get the idea.

Tango, by this point, had healed up pretty good and his hair, though cut shorter due to having had a lot of it burned off his head, looked thick and well groomed. His body had healed of the battering and the burns. He was making a bit of an effort to look strong and confident, and there was no doubt in my mind, being who he was, he would soon fit the role he was playing.

That was when we saw what looked like that painting of Venus, where she's coming out of the sea on a giant shell. This Venus was walking toward us, wearing nothing. Her golden hair was flittering in the wind, and she walked without any show of embarrassment for her nudity. She had beads woven into the hair on her head, and even into her thick pubic hair. In that moment, I think I understood, at least on some level, what men saw in such creatures, though I want to hasten to add that I prefer seal nookie. I'm merely making an anthropological statement.

I saw Tango perk, and then he began to run. The woman stood where she was and spread her arms and they came together tightly. Tango lifted her, and I knew then that the woman was Jill.

Six

This was, to say the least, unexpected.

"Oh, my world, Jilly. I failed in my quest, but you're awake. Alive."

"You are observant," Jill said. She then looked at all of us, said, "Who are your friends?"

Tango introduced us all quickly, and then said, "But how?"

"How am I alive? Well, silly boy, the disease passed. I am fortunate. I rode it out. I have been awake a long time now, waiting on your return. I was considering mounting a search party, as there are those here who knew what your quest was, but the problem was slow recovery. I woke up, and then I was as weak as a politician's promise. It took me time to manage getting up, eating breakfast, and carrying on with little more than a day of sleeping. Not in the deep coma way of before, but in a recovery way. And then one morning I woke up and felt strong, as I am now. Bottom line, dear Jack, is I am well."

Tango teared up and hugged her again, and then they kissed.

We wandered into the city to leave them alone.

———◆———

All's well that ends well someone said, and if that isn't an understatement, then nothing is.

I stayed there in the city for many sleeps, and then I decided that my original feelings that I wanted my adventuring days to be over, returned to me. I was tired. I was scarred up. I wanted to write, and I had become lazy in a fine and wonderful way.

The others had lost their watches given to them by Wells but as mine was on my sled, it had survived. Therefore, I had kept check reasonably well on the passing hours, though I certainly lost track now and then.

But, I was certain that the time for Wells to return was near.

Tango agreed to lead me back to where Time Machine had entered Down World, when I decided to leave, and hopefully catch up with Wells.

I wrote on my slate and asked Leo his plans.

"I'm staying. Place like this, you never know how things will be in the morning. And there's a little lady I got my eye on. I'm thinking I might end up with some kind of white picket fence, a yard, and a sabre tooth tiger tamed down like a house cat on the back porch. Hell, I don't really have any plans, little pal. I just know I'm not going back up there. Not to the surface world, not to that rat race, not to that place where Tuesday is going to be like Friday."

I nodded and wrote: MAKES SENSE

I wrote on my slate, inquired of Bongo Bill and Suzie Q's plans.

Their decision was easy.

They were going to stay, and not in the city. They were going to go with Rotah to the jungle, find the apes. Rotah had decided she would take back leadership of the tribe. Any naysayers, she planned to break their necks.

Simple politics. She had already set out ahead of them with instructions on how to find her and her tribe. Bongo Bill and Suzie Q, after all their experiences, were certain they could find it without any trouble. I believed they were right.

"I think we can do great things for them," Bongo Bill said.

"And he has the hots for Rotah," Suzie Q said.

"A little."

Suzie Q stared hard at him.

"All right, all right. I do have a bit of a warm feeling for her. I fear ruining their civilization by trying to advance it, but there is so much I could contribute to."

I wrote on my slate.

CIVILIZATION IS NICE IF IT ADVANCES IN A GOOD WAY

"Thank you, Ned. You have been a true friend. And if you find Wells, and you leave Down World, perhaps someday you will return."

PERHAPS.

On the day I was to leave, Jill kissed me on the nose, and so did Suzie Q, and for that matter, so did Bongo Bill. Within a short time, they planned to leave and catch up with Rotah.

Leo stuck out his hand and I put my flipper in it, and we shook. "You stay sharp, little fellow."

I nodded and smiled.

Tango loaded a pack of supplies on my sled, and then, carrying a bow and arrows in a quiver on his back, we started out.

As I guided my sled along, I looked back. For a moment, I wanted to cancel my exit, and stay, and possibly have other adventures.

But, while looking back, I ran into a tree and was knocked out of my sled. When I regained my place and pride, I looked back and shrugged, heard Bongo Bill and Suzie Q and Jill laugh.

I waved once more, and started off in pursuit of Tango, who was moving quickly along the trail out of habit. It took a lot of concentration to keep up, and to make sure when he took another path, that I was alert enough to follow.

We had a few minor events along the way, but nothing notable enough to write about. Some dinosaur stuff, a giant snake, and a couple of windy storms, but it all went smoothly enough, and after circling wide around the hill where we had first found Tango, we arrived at the spot where Time Machine was to be.

It wasn't there.

Tango said he would wait there for a dozen sleeps, but after that time it would be wise for me to return with him to the city and to the others. I felt selfish having taken him from Jill after such a long and distressing time apart, but I was glad he was there with me.

But, within only a few sleeps, there was a glow beyond the grass where we could see the great entrance from the Up World, or is it Above World? Who the fuck knows. We were inconsistent on that.

I felt a cold wind blow, and with the wind came Time Machine. It didn't just appear as I expected, but came gliding down from the surface world and landed in the spot where we had been before.

To sum it up, which at this point is best, Wells was glad to see me and I was glad to see him.

He hugged me and then Tango.

"I had every hope you would return," Wells said. "And I began to wish to come back, hoping that you had kept up with the time."

"Ned has done just that," said Tango.

"Where are the others?" Wells said. He gave me a worried look when he said that.

I glanced at Tango, and he explained all that had happened, and not too briefly, I might add.

"They are fine. They will remain here with me."

I wrote on my slate, held it up for Wells to see.

BUT I WILL GO BACK WITH YOU.

"I have thought it over," Wells said, "and we must both be writers together. I will do the serious stuff and you can write your shit."

I grinned and wrote.

I CAN'T THINK OF A BETTER IDEA.

Well, after that Tango said his goodbyes, and then me and Wells went into *Time Machine* where I was greeted by Clarence with a cup of hot chocolate, made just the way I like it.

I sat in the parlor and drank it. Wells told me of the books he had written and that had been published. He said there were copies in Time Machine's library. I wrote on my slate that I was anxious to read them, and this was true. He said he was writing a book about an invisible man next. That didn't sound as promising as the others.

THAT SOUNDS LIKE FUN. HE'S INVISIBLE, IS HE?

"He is."

We then retired to the control room, and Wells asked, "Do you remember how things work, Ned?"

I nodded.

I wrote on my slate.

LET'S JUMP TO YOUR HOME.

"And my home is now your home, little seal. You will not be seen as a pet by anyone. I will make sure of that."

I showed him my teeth in my manner of a smile, worked my section of controls with my thumbs and flippers, and Wells worked his, and, we jumped.

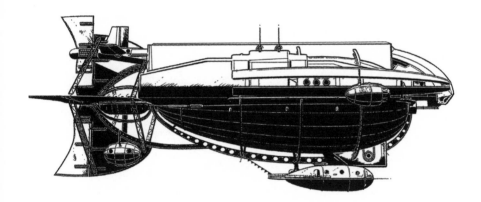